THE LAST WINDOW TO THE OLD WORLD

LENA ALISON KNIGHT

THE LAST WINDOW TO THE OLD WORLD

Copyright © 2025 by Lena Alison Knight

lenaalisonknight.com

Cover Design by: Damonza.com

All rights reserved. This book or any portion thereof may not be reproduced or used in any manner whatsoever without the express written permission of the author except for the use of brief quotations in a book review.

NO AI TRAINING: Any use of this publication to "train" generative artificial intelligence (AI) technologies to generate text is expressly prohibited.

No generative AI was used in writing this book.

❀ Created with Vellum

PROLOGUE

4073, Altren Colony

For the first time all semester, Ellie set her bag down in *Physics 181A: Introduction to Temporal Physics* without asking herself what in the universe she was doing here.

The answer to that question was obvious - getting the upper-level hard-science unit that she needed to graduate - but she still found herself asking it on a regular basis. There had been other hard-science courses she could have chosen. Ones that involved significantly less math. Why was she putting herself through this one?

She knew the answer to that too, of course. Her best friend's excitement could be infectious, and there was very little that excited Liam quite as much as time travel. When the university announced it was offering a temporal-physics course for the first time, his name had been the first on the signup list. Ellie had lasted through nearly five minutes of what she'd privately dubbed the *Liam Tsanara Weaponized Puppy Eyes*, before her name had been the second.

If she'd realized *quite* how much math this would require, she might have held out a bit longer. Liam had assured her it wouldn't be that bad; she realized later that a physics major's idea of "not that bad" might not quite line up with hers.

Today, though: today was the first and probably only time this semester she could wholeheartedly share Liam's enthusiasm for the subject. Today they weren't just sitting through a lecture on Plenisari scientists' experiences traveling through breaches in space and time to observe the past, or how calibrating the necessary device involved many dense equations.

Today, they were going to the lab to see the time machine itself.

The *temporal distortion field generator*, properly, but that was a lot of words. Much to the irritation of their professor, everyone outside the physics department simply called it a time machine.

A slim, dark-haired figure *thunked* his bag on the desk and slipped into the seat beside her.

"It's lab day!" Liam was practically glowing. "Are you excited?"

"Not as excited as you are," she replied with a grin. "But yeah, I'm pretty excited. And so's everyone else, apparently." Judging from the unusually-full lecture hall, Ellie and Liam weren't the only ones who'd specifically taken this course for a chance to see Altren's only time machine.

He leaned closer and dropped his voice a bit. "Are you going to try? Like *actually* try?"

A blush crept up her cheeks. "I mean…I know it's not going to work, of course. But this is the only time we're ever going to be this close to the time machine, much less get to actually *touch* it. Seems like a waste *not* to." Even saying it aloud sounded mildly ridiculous. If none of the University's top scientists had yet been able to use the device, a random second-year undergrad from the Agsteads wasn't going to be the one. A second-year undergrad studying *history*, no less. It felt silly - and rather presumptuous - to even make the attempt.

Liam nodded seriously at her, though, as if there were nothing silly or presumptuous in it at all. "You never know," he reminded her. "They still don't know why it works for some people and not others. We've got as good a chance as anyone."

"Do you have a memory picked out?" She knew he did, he *must*, but it was a convenient deflection from herself.

"Winning the primary-school spelling bee. Proudest moment in my nine-year-old life. I still have the medal somewhere. You?"

Her blush intensified. Of *course* Liam's anchor memory was going to be an achievement of some kind, she'd expect nothing less from the scion of one of the colony's most prominent scientist families. Hers was, well…

"When my parents brought Mikka home as a puppy," she admitted. "It was my seventh birthday and I'd wanted a dog for forever. I was so excited."

His eyes sparkled. "I hope you *do* make it, and take me through the time breach with you. That sounds like a lot more fun than a spelling bee."

She was saved from having to respond by their professor's arrival. From the wry smile playing on her lips, Dr. Banera was well aware how many of her 181A students were here for this day alone.

"Good morning, everyone, I see we have a full house today. As I'm sure you all know" - the smile deepened - "for today's section we will be conducting a visit to the physics lab to examine the temporal distortion field generator acquired by Altren University last summer. You may leave your bags here so that you aren't bumping them into anything in the lab."

The class was abuzz for the whole of the short walk to the physics lab, and the excited whispers only intensified when they were crammed into a space that most assuredly had not been built to hold eighty-five undergraduates at once. Not for the first time in her life, Ellie was grateful to be tall enough to see over most people's shoulders.

The time machine itself sat unobtrusively in the center of the room, a contraption of metal and wire that might be overlooked except that everyone was staring at it. The control console was docked on its side, still and silent as the machine itself.

Dr. Banera pitched her voice to be heard. "As you should all be aware, this is the only temporal distortion field generator currently in existence on Altren. It was assembled to the precise specifications we received from our colleagues on Plenisar, where various universities have created multiple working copies of the generator." She paced a leisurely circle around the device. "We have every reason to believe it would be as functional as the copies on Plenisar, though we have not been able to test it in practice.

"As you should all know from the reading," a stern pause, as if daring anyone present to admit they hadn't read the assignment, "it's not understood at this time why the devices will respond to some users and not others, but it appears to be a binary: it either works for a given person or it does not. And for myself and everyone else in our department, it does not.

"There have been hypotheses that the fact that no one on Altren has yet been able to use the device may point to an environmental trigger only present on Plenisar, but given that temporal distortion research is still in its infancy, it's far too early for any certainties. And unless significant advances in faster-than-light travel are made, we cannot test that hypothesis by bringing any of our Plenisari colleagues here." The wry smile was back. "Believe it or not, no one is willing to say goodbye to their homes and families and spend seventy-five years traveling through space in cryosleep, just to come here and test a hunch."

Dr. Banera lifted the control console from its dock and raised it to give the entire class a good view. There was a burst of impatient fidgeting from the students nearest Ellie. They could sense that the main event was almost here.

"As you should all be very aware by now, for those who *have* been able to operate the devices, memory has been key. Intense focus on a strong memory, combined with the calibrations performed on the device, have enabled multiple researchers to step back into the past as observers - even if the anchor memory is not their own. And so, we come to our exercise today."

The class leaned in almost as one, riveted to the console in her hand. "Everyone will get a turn with the generator, to demonstrate your calculations as per the assignment. Don't worry," she added with a laugh, "no one *expects* you to be able to use the device. You'll be graded on how well it *ought* to work, based on the calculation parameters you were given."

She winked conspiratorially. "But it never hurts to concentrate on a strong memory, just in case."

The wait felt like an eternity. Ellie and Liam were in the middle of the pack, when it came to the waiting queue, but anticipation made the minutes drag into hours. Ellie tried to distract herself by getting ahead on reading for her next class - *Century of Calamity: Plenisar and the Altren Migration, 3805-3898* - but it was hard to concentrate with the odd flutter of nerves in her belly.

Despite *knowing* it was probably futile, Ellie found herself imagining what it would be like if she *could* operate the time machine. She'd never had any desire to go into physics as a career, but back on Plenisar there was a whole new field developing for historians. Rather than simply researching in libraries and archives, "practical history" meant accompanying the field physicists on their trips to the past, to study and observe *directly*.

It wasn't a career that would ever be open to her - unless someone on Altren could work the time machine. The knowledge that that *could* happen today, no matter how unlikely, sent nervous energy humming through her veins.

Judging by how Liam was checking and rechecking calculations that he had almost certainly triple-checked the night before, he was nervous too.

At last they made it to the front, and Dr. Banera handed Ellie the device. She took a breath to steady herself, and tried to focus on details of her memory. The texture of Mikka's soft fur, her excited little barks as she ran circles around Ellie, the feeling of her rough tongue on Ellie's cheek as she leapt up to lick her face.

Ellie's own delighted laughter, the bright excitement that Mikka was hers to keep. She held the thoughts in her mind as she carefully input her calculations.

As expected, nothing happened.

Despite herself, Ellie deflated slightly. She really hadn't expected anything, but apparently some part of her was more hopeful than rational. Dr. Banera gave her work a critical examination, then scribbled something down and nodded at her to pass the device on. She handed it to over to Liam.

His elegant fingers danced over the console's keys as he input data, brow furrowed in absolute concentration. Scarcely had he entered the last number when the console's lights sprang to life.

The device vibrated slightly in his hands, and the very space in front of them distorted. The shimmering air shifted in on itself and finally coalesced into a circle, glowing softly blue as it opened to the past.

1

4077, Altren Colony
Four years later

The alarm had barely managed its first trilling notes before Ellie was out of bed and moving. She'd been awake for at least an hour, staring at her tiny studio's ceiling and waiting for the minutes to tick over until it was time to get up and ready.

So much for her fears of oversleeping. She should have realized she'd be too nervous to sleep much at all.

There really wasn't much to do to get ready. She'd chosen her clothes the night before so as to avoid indecision, and everything she needed for the day was already carefully packed and waiting by the door. A bit ironic, actually; she'd prepared everything she could last night so she wouldn't have to worry about being late this morning, and that meant she now had extra time with nothing to do *but* worry.

Ellie would be the first to admit she'd never been great at handling anticipation.

Deep breaths. It's just another day. A day that she was starting her dream job as the Altren University Temporal Distortion

Research Institute's first and only practical historian on staff. The first and only professional practical historian in all of Altren. The only feeling that could match her excitement at starting the role was her terror that she wouldn't live up to it.

Deep breaths.

A bright *ping* announced an incoming message. The code for the West 3 Agricultural Steading messaging center number lit up her handheld.

>*Have a great first day, sweetheart. We're so proud of you!*

Ellie's eyes burned slightly. It was *early* in West Ag 3, even by farmer standards. Her mom must have set a special alarm to make sure she got down to the public terminal to send the message before Ellie left for work.

Ellie blinked suddenly wet eyes against a surprise wave of homesickness. It seemed strange to even call it that - the Agsteads hadn't been home for over six years, and they probably never would be again. Not since she'd beaten the odds, and become the only West 3 Secondary student in her year to qualify for Altren University.

And now she was employed there. The thought jolted her back into the present, and Ellie dashed off a quick reply as she powered through the rest of her breakfast. Her mom wouldn't see it until her next trip to check the terminal, of course, but at least there would be a return message waiting for her when she did.

That homesick feeling intensified as she hit send. Back when she lived in West Ag 3, Ellie could never have imagined having her own device, to send and receive messages *wherever she wanted*. Now here she was, tapping out messages on her University-issued handheld like it wasn't a big deal at all.

Speaking of, she needed to be on her way to the University itself. The only thing more nerve-wracking than her first day at AUTDRI would be riding in alone - which was exactly what was going to happen if she didn't get moving. A quick glance around to ensure she had everything - not that it was easy to lose things in a micro-studio apartment - and she was out the door.

Altren's binary suns were still low in the sky, and the early-spring chill found her wishing her blazer were a bit more functional. Ellie made her way down to the metro station at a fast clip, which backfired when she arrived early for her train and then had to wait shivering on the platform.

She slipped her phone out, more to distract herself from how cold she was than anything.

>*You're getting on the 708, right?*

It took a few tries to get the message down. She wasn't a fast handheld-typer under the best of circumstances, and the cold numbing her fingers certainly wasn't helping hit the right keys.

Barely ten seconds later Liam's answering message popped up.

>>*On my way to the station. Hold me a seat?*

> *If there's any left to hold.*

She eyed the crowded platform dubiously. One of the biggest things she was going to miss about grad school was the flexibility to *not* be on the metro when everyone else on Altren was trying to get into work.

The train glided serenely into the station, at odds with the impatient commuters that lined the platform. Luck was with her - it came to a stop with a door directly in front of where she was standing. A few sharp elbows later and her goal was achieved: two seats on the upper deck of the train, one shamelessly occupied by her satchel. She pretended not to notice the dark looks thrown her way.

>*Got one! Upper deck, car 21. Look for the asshole leaving her bag on a seat that everyone else is glaring at.*

>>*Your sacrifice is appreciated.*

>*You could show your appreciation with sweetbuns.*

While Ellie envied many things about Liam's apartment - that it was closer to the university, that the balcony had a view, that it had more than one room - his proximity to the best bakery this side of the city was what she envied the most. More than once, she'd half-seriously considered if paying 20% more in rent was worth it for access to Sunrise Bread pastries straight out of the oven.

So far the math on that one hadn't penciled out. But hey, if things went well at the Institute? Who knew. Maybe she'd even get an apartment where the bed didn't fold out of the wall.

She'd been doing a decent job of distracting herself from being nervous, but the thought brought it all immediately rushing back. *Dammit Ellie. Breathe.*

The train pulled to another gradual stop, and a low buzz of conversation filled the car as more people crowded in. Ellie kept a light hand on her bag as she scanned the oncoming riders, cheeks heating slightly at the flagrant violation of metro etiquette. Usually she tried to be a polite, considerate rider.

Just not today.

She finally spotted him carefully elbowing his way through the crowd. Ellie waited until he drew up beside her to take her bag and scoot closer to the window. Liam dropped into the seat she'd just vacated with a grin.

"Thank you for your service," he said with a wink, and pressed a still-warm bag with the Sunrise logo into her hand. "Hopefully this didn't get too squished."

Squished or not, the sweetbun still smelled heavenly - cardamom and butter and fresh-baked dough. She took a deep breath just to savor the scent, then tore into it like a hungry wolf.

Well, a wolf who was being careful not to get sugar all over its face and the most professional attire it owned.

"Mm," she said around bites. "Hardly squished at all. Still perfect. Thank you."

"I figured it's a special occasion, we could both use some extra morale."

Now that she took the time to actually *look* at Liam, Ellie couldn't help but notice he'd put in extra effort today as well. He was sharply dressed in a blazer and slacks, and his smooth black hair was styled back immaculately enough that she was willing to bet it had taken multiple tries. The Liam sitting next to her looked poised, professional, and certainly not like someone she had last seen trying to slur his way through an explanation of dimensional theory after several rounds of shots at their grad party.

Instead, he looked like the Tsanara heir; scion of one of the colony's founding families, great-grandson of the University's first chemistry chair, and Altren's only field-capable temporal physicist. He looked like he belonged exactly where they were going, and for a moment she could still feel the mud of West Ag 3 clinging to her shoes.

He leaned forward with one of those exuberant grins, and the spell broke. The Tsanara heir vanished, and she was sitting beside her best friend again.

"Can you believe this is finally happening?" He moved as if to run a hand through his hair, jerking back at the last minute before he could muss it. "Starting at AUTDRI, I mean. It almost doesn't feel real."

"It doesn't," she agreed, downing the last of her sweetbun. "But here we are on this train first thing in the morning."

"So it *better* be real," he laughed. "I'm going to be really upset if I got up for the 708 and this was all a big mistake."

She smiled back, trying to ignore the sudden twinge. There was no chance of *that* happening. Liam had had a role earmarked at the University since that fateful day in their under-grad lab. In a very real sense, it was only because of Liam Tsanara that AUTDRI existed at all. There was no one else on Altren capable of working the distortion generator.

There were, on the other hand, quite a few people qualified for the role of field historian, many of whom came from presti-gious families with close connections to the university. Ellie's grades had been at the top of the class, her professors had given her glowing recommendations, and she knew she'd aced the interviews at AUTDRI. Still, the realist in her had to acknowledge that that hadn't been the *whole* reason she'd been selected.

AUTDRI would likely have interviewed her regardless, but they'd *hired* her because they were hiring Liam, and Liam wanted to work with Ellie.

She kept the thought to herself. Liam would tell her she was being silly, that she had earned every bit of her place here, that she was the best and brightest in her young field. She appreciated his efforts to encourage her, she really did. It meant a lot knowing that her best friend was in her corner, come what may. But this was something that Liam, latest in a long line of high-achieving Tsanaras, didn't understand. *Couldn't* understand.

This was her chance to contribute to time research in her own right, to establish herself as valuable for more reason than simply that AUTDRI's only field-capable temporal physicist preferred to work with her. To prove that a girl from the Agsteads *did* belong there, and that her most significant accomplishment wasn't accidentally bumping her lunch tray into Liam in their first week of undergrad.

Even if it was just to herself.

"Ellie? You doing alright?" Liam's light touch on her arm broke her out of her thoughts. "You have that look like you need someone to remind you that you've got nothing to worry about and AUTDRI is lucky to have you."

Her lips curved of their own accord. "You know me too well. I guess it's a little early to be worrying about performance reviews before we even get in the building."

"Just a little," he concurred. "Let's agree to hold off on worrying about that until at least after orientation."

Before she could respond, the train's chime echoed through the car. "*University Station,*" a soothing synthetic voice announced. "*Now arriving, University Station.*"

She hopped up, ignoring the renewed surge of anxiety in her gut. "Ready or not, that's our cue."

———

The AUTDRI building was just as unimpressive as on her first visit, the one where she'd interviewed in the lone, windowless conference room wedged in beside the lobby. In fact, if Ellie were being uncharitable, she might describe AUTDRI's office as *a glorified shed.*

It was one of the older buildings in the University's science cluster, possibly the oldest in its current form. It had originally been built as a lab and passed between departments for the last several decades. Most recently the experimental physics department had used it at as auxiliary lab space, but when they moved on to newer and better facilities, the structure had been hastily refitted as a headquarters for AUTDRI.

A bit disappointing, but it wasn't a huge surprise that the University hadn't bothered to build AUTDRI a shiny new office. Temporal physics exploration might be the cutting edge of science, but the lack of field-capable researchers on Altren meant that none of that groundbreaking advancement had been happening here. If Liam hadn't signed on to join the future AUTDRI when they were still in grad school, it probably never would have been established at all.

No pressure.

The door creaked irritably as they went inside. The office's interior wasn't much of an improvement. The front doors opened into a small makeshift lobby, made up of a threadbare couch and battered, currently-unoccupied reception desk, over carpet that looked like it might well date from the University's founding. Someone had tried valiantly to modernize the space, but their budget had apparently only extended to cover a pair of sleek floor lamps and a few potted plants. Unfortunately, the out-of-place new items only underlined the outdated shabbiness of the rest of the office. At least the plants looked well cared for.

The lobby was also empty, with only the sharp click of a large wall clock to break the silence. Several minutes passed.

"So," Liam said finally. "Do you think there's a bell we ring, or - "

The double doors to the rest of the office burst open to admit a vaguely familiar young woman pushing a mail cart. She squeaked and rushed over as she saw them, abandoning the cart to its fate.

"You're here! I wasn't expecting you this early!"

Ellie's glance shifted to the wall clock. It was now more than five after their scheduled arrival time.

"I mean, you're early, that's great, they're waiting for you, we can get started right away-" she cut herself off. "Actually, I guess you still have to do the paperwork…You can fill out paperwork fast, right?"

A brief whirlwind of forms later, they were finally escorted to the Director of AUTDRI's office. Dr. Renton wasn't alone.

"Greetings and welcome, it's very exciting to finally have you both on staff." Renton rose to shake both their hands with gusto, though a tightness around her eyes belied her enthusiasm. The look intensified as she gestured at the man sitting beside her desk. "Have you both met Chancellor Felden?"

2

The University's Chancellor regarded them coolly. He was a serious-looking man, in late middle age, with dark brown hair turning silver. He was also quite definitely not the Chancellor they had met previously.

"I don't think I've had the pleasure," he answered before they could speak. His tone indicated it was not a pleasure in the slightest. "Dr. Perrel Felden. I took over as Chancellor from Dr. Tarethen over the summer."

Ah. It was Dr. Tarethen that Ellie had met before, at the reception to celebrate the founding of AUTDRI. Chancellor Tarethen had been the one to sign off on the initiative, and Ellie remembered her enthusiasm when she spoke to Liam about her hopes for the Institute and its research.

Chancellor Felden looked notably *less* enthused.

"As you're aware, Chancellor," Renton picked up briskly, "Dr. Tsanara is joining us as Altren's only field-capable temporal physicist, and at a most fortuitous time. Or I suppose," she added with a tight smile at Liam, "the fortuitous time is here because *you* are." She waved for them to have a seat. Ellie carefully perched herself on a questionably-stable folding chair across from Renton's desk and prayed it didn't collapse on her as the Director was talking.

"AUTDRI has just been presented with a once-in-a-lifetime opportunity. Once-in-*several*-lifetimes, more precisely. Stella Hartford has volunteered to work with us on a field expedition."

She paused at their blank expressions. "You may be more familiar with her sister Maria."

Liam started beside her, and Ellie barely kept her own surprise in check. *Of course* they were familiar with Maria Hartford. There wasn't a child on either planet who wasn't raised on stories of the Savior of Plenisar, the brilliant biotechnologist whose terraforming breakthroughs had rejuvenated the pollution-ravaged planet back to a healthy environment for human habitation. Her work was intrinsic to their own history as well; Altren had been founded as a refuge of last resort, for however many people could be transported over before Plenisar died completely. It was thanks to Maria Hartford's success that their world was a backwater curio, rather than the final tattered remnants of the human race.

No one had ever mentioned her having a sister - much less a sister who lived on *Altren*.

Some of Ellie's thoughts must have leaked onto her face. "Stella Hartford has always been very private," Dr. Renton noted. "She came to Altren as a teenager with her family on the last colony ship from Plenisar, before anyone knew that the terraforming project would be successful. She's lived very quietly here, and avoided any sort of spotlight related to her family. Now that Altren is capable of conducting temporal field research, however, she has expressed her willingness to participate in a time study.

"As you know, the last colony ship arrived here over seventy years ago. Ms. Hartford was one of the youngest onboard, and she is now the only person from that journey still alive today on Altren." Dr. Renton paused a bit to let the implication sink in.

"And thus also, the only person alive on Altren who remembers Plenisar."

Liam's sharp intake of breath echoed against her own shock. Was Renton really saying - ?

She was. "The plan is to make use of Ms. Hartford's memories to power the time-distortion array, and ultimately make a jump back to her memories of Plenisar. We intend to also make several smaller jumps to the time after her arrival on Altren, to gather data about lived experience in the early days of the colony." Renton shot a glance at the Chancellor sitting beside her. "This project provides an opportunity to secure *invaluable* historical data." Felden's lips pursed slightly but he said nothing.

"We will be gathering data from the early days of Altren," Renton repeated, "but Plenisar is the main objective. Specifically, Maria Hartford's Planetary Address. Stella was in the audience, right before her departure for Altren. If her living memory is as strong as she claims, you will be able to witness the Address in person. That is the chief goal of this project."

Ellie was starting to feel a bit lightheaded. Sure, why not - they were already going to the past of another planet, to see a legend in the flesh. Why not also witness her most renowned public speech, that inspired a flagging Plenisar to fight for its own survival and lodged itself indelibly in the collective consciousness of two worlds. They were going to be in the audience for something Ellie had written an essay about in primary school.

This day was already going unexpected places, and it wasn't even midmorning yet.

"I hope you both understand the magnitude of this opportunity." Renton met both their eyes in turn. "This is about more than the chance to observe a significant historical figure. This is our last window to the old world. We are going to attempt to go back *150 years,* and it's only possible because Stella Hartford spent half that time in cryosleep. No one alive on Plenisar today is old enough to have lived through the events we will witness.

"Furthermore, besides just the amount of time, there is the matter of *space*. We will be traveling further into the past, and further from our location, than anyone before has ever been able to attempt. This is an opportunity that may never recur, and that could only *ever* arise on Altren."

She added the last a bit forcefully, and Ellie got the impression Renton wasn't speaking only to them. Her unspoken meaning, too, was clear. This was an opportunity to win the respect of the universities back on Plenisar, with a feat the Plenisari could literally never match. Not so long as the distortion generators required a living memory.

Up to this point Chancellor Felden had listened without speaking. Now, however, he leaned in.

"I'll be upfront here that I would have preferred a more experienced team for a project of this importance." His eyes briefly cut to Ellie. "At the very least a more seasoned historian, since the physicist portion is out of our hands."

"Dr. Nelseren has had more hands-on experience in time travel than anyone else on Altren," Liam answered coolly before Ellie could react. "The first time I opened a distortion portal outside my own memories, it was powered by hers."

"The responsibilities of the project go further than simply stepping through a glowing circle. However, the Director," he nodded toward Renton, whose lips had compressed, "concluded that, coupled with your existing rapport, Dr. Nelseren's graduate field work and strong faculty recommendations were qualification enough to hire into a new position, instead of pulling from our existing staff." His tone made clear that he had not shared that conclusion.

Ellie wasn't sure how to respond to that. Nor did he seem to expect her to - Felden wasn't even looking at her. She hated that she didn't know what to say, hated that this discussion of her role felt like a negotiation between Felden and Liam, and that she might as well not be in the room. Even Renton, who'd ultimately made the decision to hire her, was watching Liam during the entire exchange. Suns, this felt like a metaphor for her whole career.

And if you don't at least try *to fight your own battles, that's never going to change.*

She found her voice. "I assure you, Chancellor, I take this opportunity very seriously and I will deliver what's needed for the Hartford project." Heads turned towards her as if in surprise she'd spoken. She did her best not to react. "I would be happy to discuss my methodology in greater detail, if that would help address your concerns."

Felden made an uninterested noise and leaned back in his seat. "My biggest concerns are with the amount of resources being invested in this initiative. I understand that Chancellor Tarethen was intrigued by the work being done on Plenisar in temporal physics, and the science coming out of that field is certainly interesting to study." The *but* that was coming was almost palpable.

"However, Plenisar's existential crisis is behind it. Ours is still looming in the distance. I question Tarethen's decision to allocate funds and components, that could go to the electronic synthesis effort, into an emerging field with no practical applications.

"It is not the decision I would have made." He let that pronouncement settle for a moment before continuing. "However, given that these resources have already been spent, it seems an even greater waste to cancel the initiative with no results, particularly given the amount of public interest in this research." His lips drew down on the last words, as if he took the average person's interest in time travel as a personal affront. "I expect that you will make every effort to deliver results on time and on budget."

He rose then and gave them each a nod, then left the office. Silence bloomed in his wake.

Renton reached over to give the door a light shove. It clicked closed, and she turned to face them both with an air of getting down to business.

"I see no point in talking around this: as you can see, we are under a great deal of scrutiny from the university administration. The previous chancellor was very interested in exploration and discovery, which is a large part of why she approved funding for AUTDRI once we had a path to field capability. It's also why her retirement comes at a very unfortunate time for us. Chancellor Felden has spent his entire career in Material Science, and he is very focused on solving for our current electronics problems.

"Which are very important," she added. "It may well be that that focus is what we need in these times. But I believe, and Chancellor Tarethen agreed, that it would be a mistake to sacrifice every other endeavor in pursuit of that solution. Impractical things like art and exploration are what make us human. But." She steepled her fingers on her desk. "That does not change our reality, which is that Chancellor Felden will ultimately make the decision if we will continue with our work."

Renton looked between them, face deadly serious. "I know you are new to this organization and these roles, but there is no time for a learning curve. This opportunity will not come around again. Unless there are significant advances in faster-than-light travel in our lifetimes, Stella Hartford may be the last person on Altren to *ever* see Plenisar. And she is ninety-two years old. If this isn't done right, we won't get another chance, and Felden will get the reason he wants to shut us down. Do you both understand me?"

They both nodded silently. Renton rose to usher them out of her office.

"You'll be working with Dahlia as your project manager, she should stop by to introduce herself later. Please don't hesitate to ask her any questions. I look forward to seeing your work." The door closed behind them.

No pressure, indeed.

———

Liam maintained his composure as they left the uncomfortable meeting, nearly until they reached the small nook where their desks had been tucked away. "Shoved in sideways" might actually be a better descriptor; the space was tight enough that they essentially had *one* desk with two chairs at it. Once they'd made it to that desk, however, his excitement finally bubbled over.

"The *Planetary Address*. Ellie, we're going to see the *Planetary Address*, live, *on Plenisar*. We're going to *see* Maria Hartford, right in front of us, on humanity's planet of origin."

"We are," she agreed with a slight laugh. "And did you miss the part where the new head of the university flat-out told us he didn't think AUTDRI should exist, and then threatened us if we screw this up?"

"Oh, I caught it. But since we're not *going* to screw it up, we've got nothing to worry about." He leaned in, eyes aglow. "We may be junior researchers on paper, but we're also the only ones in the building who have regularly traveled back in time. The *only* paper to come out of Altren, based on *actual* experience with time distortion fields? It's got *our* names on it, not anyone here."

"That wasn't enough for the new chancellor, apparently. At least not for my part." She tried and failed to keep the irritation out of her tone.

"I don't think he even understands your part. He wanted to pull your role 'from existing staff,' remember? Never mind that the existing staff has basically *zero* experience doing temporal field work. He's just bitter he has to pay our salaries. If anyone on *existing staff* could work the distortion array, he'd be saying the same thing about me."

He'd be more willing to hire the Tsanara scion than a nobody from West Ag 3. She kept the thought to herself; that wasn't Liam's fault, and she appreciated what he was trying to do. Her insecurities wouldn't help either of them.

She was rescued from having to respond by a sharp knock on the wall. Standing in what Ellie was already starting to think of as the "door" was a petite woman roughly their age, with thick-rimmed glasses and eye-catching red streaks in her dark hair. She held out a hand.

"Dr. Liam Tsanara and Dr. Elinor Nelseren, I take it?" She didn't wait for them to confirm. "I'm Dahlia Tiri, AUTDRI's lead project manager." Her lips quirked. "And only project manager. Which means I'm your PM for the Hartford case. Bet you weren't expecting *that* on your first day, were you?"

Ellie decided she liked Dahlia. "This whole day has been full of surprises," she admitted. "But it's certainly an exciting start to our roles here."

"Fantastic! I'm glad you're excited." Dahlia *thunked* a heavy folder on the desk. "Because the timeline for the project is, how can I put this, extremely aggressive. I think Director Renton wants to lock this thing down before either Stella Hartford or Chancellor Felden can change their minds."

Liam raised his eyebrows. "How aggressive are we talking?"

"Well, when Stella first agreed, they had me spec out a project timeline based on what I thought was reasonable for the scope. I presented it to Renton, and she cut it in half. So…"

Dahlia flipped the folder open and an unrolled a long, rectangular sheet of paper with timeline and dates drawn in heavy ink. "We're here." She pointed to a spot roughly 10% down the line, where "Field Team Starts" was circled several times. "We're hoping to do two preparatory jumps to explore some of Stella's memories of life on early Altren, and also to build a working relationship as we ramp up to Planetary Address. Which has the two of you on Plenisar in…" her finger slid to the other end of the timeline. "A little over three months."

The air whooshed out of her lungs. Three months to prepare for a jump of that magnitude, with *two others* in the runup…

Liam's finger stabbed down on one of the nearer points. "The first jump is in *two and a half weeks?*"

"That's the plan," Dahlia confirmed. "Of course we don't know what it's going to *be* yet, but that's what Dr. Nelseren is going to find out tomorrow." She turned to Ellie. "That reminds me, we've already made the appointment with Stella's care home, they're expecting you around midday tomorrow."

Oh suns above.

"Got it," she echoed weakly. Well, she'd wanted an opportunity to prove herself.

Something must have shown on her face anyway, because Dahlia beamed at her. "Cheer up! It could be worse. We could be trying to do the first jump *this week.*"

"Was that discussed?"

Dahlia's laugh bordered on a snicker. "Mm, yeah, more than once. Fortunately for both our time and our credibility with Stella, we know from the Plenisari chronomancers' data that a jump like this is going to require considerable prep work in order to set *our* chronomancer up for success."

Liam's posture stiffened beside her, and Ellie inwardly groaned. The *c-word* was a surefire way to get his hackles up.

"Thank you, but I'm a *scientist*. That's all."

"That's *not* all, or you wouldn't be here." Dahlia didn't sound offended, more simply matter-of-fact. "Most of us can't rip holes in the fabric of space and time, time-distortion device or not. You can. That's something special, no matter what you want to call it."

"And you want to call it chronomancy?"

Dahlia shrugged. "It's as good a term as any. People have been looking for a rational explanation for fifteen years, and nobody's found one. At some point you need to follow where the evidence is pointing."

"Seriously though, *magic?* You really believe humans just suddenly developed supernatural powers to go back in time?"

"Maybe humans *always* had supernatural powers, and just

didn't have the means to use them until now. World's full of mysteries, Dr. Tsanara."

Liam looked like he still wanted to argue the point. Meanwhile, Ellie was pretty sure that getting in a fight with their new PM on their first day of work was an objectively terrible idea.

"It's a good thing you've already gotten a start on planning the prep work," she cut in. "Can you walk us through it?"

"That's why I'm here," Dahlia replied agreeably. She seemed wholly unruffled by Liam's chronomancy skepticism. "So I'm guessing Renton dropped the project on you, gave you some portentous rumblings about how important it is, and then kicked you out of her office with no details, am I right?"

Ellie's inclination to like Dahlia intensified. "That's an accurate summary, yes."

"Well then." Dahlia slid a few more papers out of her folder. "Let's go week by week."

The to-do list would have been long enough for just the Plenisar jump; with two others on schedule, it was dizzying. There were physical locations to research, dense calculations to be done for the device calibration, nostalgia-invoking items to acquire and multiple preparatory interviews to conduct with Stella herself, starting with Ellie's appointment the next day.

"At this stage it's mostly a meet-and-greet," Dahlia explained. "Introduce yourself, get Stella talking, maybe identify a couple of points that could be good candidates for the initial jumps before we work up to the Address. You'll have several sessions to get more detail on specific memories, so don't worry about getting too deep in the first visit."

Dahlia tapped the top of Ellie's notebook, interrupting her rapid scribbling. "And off the record," the PM added with a meaningful look, "try to get a sense of her mental condition, and if she's together enough to actually do this. She's ninety-two. She seemed sharp enough when she talked to the Chancellor, but you'll be the first one to talk to her in-depth."

Ellie resumed scribbling. "Introduce myself, discuss strong

memories, evaluate if she's sound enough for this to work. Got it."

"Oh, and while you're there, it would be great to get a sense for her physical state also. Maybe get an idea for what we'll need to do to accommodate her."

"Accommodate her?" Ellie's brow wrinkled. Powering the machine was a mental exercise. Physically, all Stella would have to do was sit there.

"Didn't Dr. Renton mention that? It was Stella's condition for working with us. She wants to go with you, when you go back to watch Maria's speech."

<h1 style="text-align:center">3</h1>

Stella Hartford resided in a rest home nestled in one of the lightly-trafficked suburbs on Altren City's northern edge. There were still trains that went up to the area, of course - Altren City had been designed around mass transit, and there was nowhere in the city that didn't have at least *some* connection to the hub. "Accessible," however, was not the same thing as "convenient."

Few people traveled frequently from the business centers up to the north neighborhoods; when they did, the city planners seemed to have assumed that they weren't terribly concerned about speed. The thrice-daily train to Blossom Heights was small, mostly empty, and in no particular hurry to get where it was going. Ellie had her pick of seats, and settled in to spend the next hour of her life on a slow-motion tour of the north city.

It really wasn't all that bad; the north city was tranquil and actually rather charming, or at least so it looked from the window. She'd never really had cause to come up this way in the six years she'd lived in Altren City. The train plodded past small local eateries and bright neighborhood gardens, and Ellie could see why Stella had retired to a home in Blossom Heights. It seemed like a delightful area, so long as you didn't have any pressing need to get anywhere else.

Her handheld pinged softly as a text from Liam popped onto the screen.

>*How's the 339? Got the entire car to yourself?*

>>*Pretty much. It's me and this one older lady, and she hasn't looked up from her knitting since I got on. I'm taking up two whole seats, just for giggles. Not so bad though, I'm basically getting paid to stare out the window until we finally make it to Stella's.*

>*I'm kinda jealous. I'm getting a start on the calibration equations, and riding the train to nowhere sounds a lot more fun.*

Ellie smiled at her handheld. He might put on a show of complaining, but they both knew it was just a show. Liam loved the complex mathematics that went into preparing the time distortion device for a jump.

Even after years of working together on time projects, she still didn't *really* understand how that part of the process worked. The distortion devices needed strong memories, and especially nostalgia, to generate the portals back to a specific time, but it wasn't *all* they needed. Getting the device focused enough to generate a time distortion field in the right temporal space meant lots of calibrating, which meant lots of math. She'd barely squeaked by with a C- in their fateful undergrad course.

Fortunately, no one really *expected* the project's historian to understand the technical bits. All she had to do was be ready to document whatever lay on the portal's other side.

>>*I'm really curious to meet Stella. Definitely didn't see it coming, that she'd request to go with us on the Address jump.*

>*From what Dahlia said it was more of a demand. We need her to go, she won't help unless she can go too.*

>>*It just seems weird. Most people are a little more freaked out about jumping into a hole in space and time, using tech that didn't exist twenty years ago.*

>*Maybe she has a hidden daredevil streak.*

Another message from Liam popped up, before she had a chance to respond.

>It kinda makes sense though, right? This is the first chance anyone on Altren has had to go back in time, and she's running out of time herself. If she's 92 she can't afford to wait until the field is more settled.

>>I guess the big question is, why is she so eager to go back that she'd make it a condition of working with the department?

And the only one with the answer to that question was Stella herself.

———

The attendant knocked lightly on the suite door. "Ms. Hartford? I have Dr. Nelseren from AUTDRI here to see you." A strong, clear voice gave affirmation through the door, and Ellie was escorted inside to come face to face with Stella.

The oldest woman on Altren stared back at her from her seat on a bright-patterned settee in the middle of the room. A walker positioned in easy reach suggested her age was catching up with her physically, but her eyes were sharp as she looked Ellie up and down. She didn't look terribly pleased to see her.

"You're not the right one," Stella pronounced without preamble. "The chronomancer was a boy."

So it was going to be one of *those* interviews.

"My colleague Dr. Tsanara is the lead temporal physicist for this project, yes," she answered, keeping her voice agreeable. "I'm Dr. Elinor Nelseren, lead practical historian. I'm here for our preliminary interview to help gather the information we need to make the time jumps." Usually, *Dr. Nelseren* still sounded weird to her ears, but at the moment Ellie intended to cling to its aura of serious respectability like a shield.

A shield she could bludgeon people with, if it came down to it.

But Stella didn't argue, simply pursed her lips together and nodded. "They said we'd need to do a few meetings first, before you can open the time portals. But I was expecting the boy."

"I'm sorry to disappoint you," Ellie lied. "But the information we collect today and in our future interviews will be important to Dr. Tsanara's work with the time distortion device." Then, because she wasn't afraid to issue a bribe - "If everything goes well, Dr. Tsanara will come with me to prepare for the final jump to watch the Planetary Address. Bringing multiple people through the time distortion requires extra consideration, and it works more easily if everyone going through has a relationship with the temporal physicist." Out of loyalty she didn't say *the chronomancer.*

"So Dr. Tsanara will certainly want to talk with you beforehand, since you're going to come through with us..." Ellie let the unspoken question hang there, hoping Stella would pick it up.

She didn't.

"I certainly am." Her tone was matter-of-fact. "Well all right then, what do you need to know?"

Ellie took her response as an opportunity to arrange herself on the chair opposite Stella's settee. "To start, we can talk about your experiences at the Planetary Address, and then after that I'd like to discuss some of your most vivid memories here on Altren..."

In the first fifteen minutes of their interview, any concerns Dahlia might have had about Stella's mental acuity were laid to rest. She recalled watching the Address on her last day on Plenisar in crisp detail. Something still felt...odd, about her whole recital, in a way that Ellie couldn't really identify. But Stella's attention to detail was impeccable, particularly given how much time had passed, and Ellie could hardly raise some vague *feeling* as a cause for concern. All the *actual* requirements were met.

She marked down that there were no red flags on being able to power the Plenisar jump.

With the most important part down first, they spent the next hours talking through the most memorable parts of Stella's life on Altren. Her rocky introduction to Stella soon faded into sheer fascination, as Ellie focused on furiously taking down all that she could. She had a recorder, of course, but she found writing things down in the moment helped her remember. And there was just so *much* here. Even if there were no time travel involved, Stella had lived through some of the most significant events in human history, and her memory was *excellent*.

The knock on the door almost startled Ellie out of her chair. It was the nurse from earlier, letting them know that it was time for Stella's afternoon medicine, and that visitor hours were ending soon for non-family. Ellie blinked in disbelief at her phone; several hours had passed, and she was overdue to check in with Dahlia.

She was also overdue to leave in general. If she didn't hurry, she was going to miss the third of the thrice-daily trains back to the city center, and wouldn't *that* be a mess.

Ellie said her goodbyes to Stella and reconfirmed their next interview date, then she was out the door. The suns were significantly lower in the sky than when she'd arrived, further emphasizing that she'd been at the rest home longer than anticipated. Fortunately, it was a short walk to the train station, and Ellie could hustle when she needed to. All the same, she didn't relax until she'd settled into her seat for the plodding journey home.

A message from Dahlia was waiting for her.

>*So how'd it go? You get started OK?*

>>*Better than OK, I was with her for almost four hours. Mentally she's in great shape, we should have no trouble using her memory for the portal. Also got a list of target memories for the earlier jumps, a lot of great stuff in there.*

>*Any highlights?*

>>*The Last Landing, for one. I know the Planetary Address is the big prize here, but I'd argue the Landing is almost as good. We'll never get another shot at THAT, either.*

>*Fantastic. Pull off a 2 for 1 combo on big historic events, and*

maybe AUTDRI can get enough funding to buy chairs that don't wobble.

The message startled a laugh out of her; fortunately, the train was as empty as its morning counterpart had been.

Another message popped up before she could respond.

>You feel like you have what you need to decide on our first jump?

>>Yes. I need to organize my notes, then I'll pull the most promising bits for our meeting tomorrow. Once we decide on our first objective I'll hit the Archives for more detail.

>Perfect, keep me informed. I'll walk you through all the forms I need filled out once you're back in the office.

Forms. Delightful.

Her handheld pinged again with another message. She started mentally composing an affirmative that she'd get all the forms done, but to her surprise it wasn't a follow-up from Dahlia. Rather, it was from a bank office's message terminal.

>El and Shan: DoubleStar Noodles @ 19:00? Need to hear about Ellie's first day. - Kira

Ellie's stomach growled, and she was abruptly reminded how little she'd eaten today. Her interview with Stella had gone on much longer than planned. And DoubleStar was one of her few favorite haunts that was actually near her apartment - which was perfect, because she'd had about all the metro travel today she could handle.

Besides, she reflected with a grin, if she didn't meet her friends for dinner, they might well show at her doorstep demanding details on her start at AUTDRI. Kira had already been remarkably patient in waiting *this* long.

>>Sounds amazing. On a train back from Blossom Heights, meet you both there as soon as soon as I get back to the neighborhood. Assuming none of us dies of old age before then.

The train came to a wheezing halt at yet another empty station, sitting patiently for a full thirty seconds in case any passengers suddenly materialized - just as it did at every single station on the north line. Ellie settled back in her seat, and let thoughts of heaping DoubleStar noodle bowls give her strength.

The part about dying of old age had only *sort of* been a joke.

———

Kira and Shana were already seated by the time she finally made it to DoubleStar. Kira waved her over with gusto.

"There's our trailblazer! First practical historian on Altren, right here." Kira must have come straight from work also - she was still in a suit and jacket that screamed *financial sector.* "Got any record-breaking projects on your plate yet?"

"Let her sit *down*, Kira. And maybe eat before you start grilling her." Shana's admonishment carried the quiet authority of what Ellie thought of as her *teacher voice.* Even after several years, it was still strange to think about her mild-mannered university roommate wrangling secondary-school students into understanding Altren's history and government.

"All right, fine, you get a solid three bites before I ask another question." Kira grinned and pushed a bowl towards her. "We went ahead and got you your usual."

It smelled *heavenly.* Ellie managed to grunt out a thank you before shamelessly shoveling noodles into her mouth.

"Okay, maybe more than three bites," Kira laughed. "Shan, while we're waiting, what were you saying about the computer lab?"

"It's closing," Shana answered, a note of resignation in her voice. "We'll keep one of the broken-down desk stations as an exhibit piece, but the rest are getting folded into the University archives. Too valuable to waste on secondary school students."

"Did they *say* that?"

"No, it was the usual about resource conservation, but we all knew what they meant. And?" Shana sighed and spread her hands in a gesture of frustration. "They're not *wrong.* We're still going to offer Computer Specialist as an elective course, but it's all textbooks and theory now. Anyone who wants to pursue it as a career path will have to wait until university for hands-on experience."

They fell quiet for moment. Nobody said it, but Ellie knew they were all thinking the same thing: there would be decreasing need for career technicians, as the amount of functioning Plenisari tech inexorably diminished.

Altren had everything you could want to support human life: a compatible atmosphere, broad temperate zones, vast swathes of rich soil well-suited to agriculture. What it did *not* have were several minerals that were essential for manufacturing the kind of advanced electronics that had existed on Plenisar. Given the bleak situation on Plenisar at the time, it was understandable that ensuring access to those minerals hadn't been a priority versus ensuring the survival of humanity at all. But they *had* survived, and now the very last reserves of materials brought from Plenisar were nearly exhausted, with no alternatives in sight.

"Still," Kira said finally. "Weird to think that we're going to be the last generation that learned how to operate computers in school."

Ellie took another big bite of noodles to avoid needing to say anything. *They* learned basic computer operations in school, in that lab that was finally closing down. The Agstead schools hadn't seen a computer in decades. When she'd first needed to use one of the workstations in the University library, Liam had had to show her how.

He'd been kind about it, just like Kira and Shana would be kind about it if she said anything now. And it wasn't as if there was really anything to hide. They both knew she was originally from West Ag 3, and they'd never tried to make her feel lesser for it. Still. She didn't want to make things awkward. She focused instead on the eminently safe subject of demolishing her noodles.

Which did not go unnoticed. "All right, it's been way more

than three bites, and I'm dying over here." Kira braced her hands on the table as if to steady herself. "Ellie. First day of work. Tell us everything."

She did. They both made disgusted noises when she got to the part about Felden's opinion on her role.

"He didn't even interview you. How can he have an opinion on your competence?"

"I think it's rolled up in his general opinion of AUTDRI." It felt less personal now, with time and space between her and Felden, and she could recount the story without feeling the same sting. "Though somehow I don't think he would have objected as vocally if it were just Liam they hired."

Kira made a face. "Well, maybe. The Feldens and the Tsanaras have always kind of had a rivalry going on." She rolled her eyes. "Not enough to be *one of* the richest and most important families in Altren, one of them needs to be *the* most important. It's a whole thing at parties sometimes."

Shana's tone was dry. "Ellie and I don't get invited to those kinds of parties, Kira."

Their friend's cheeks pinked. "Well, you're not missing much."

Nothing except the chance to mingle with the kind of people who run the whole colony. Ellie exchanged the barest glance with Shana; neither of them said it. Kira got even more awkward about this kind of thing than Liam did, even if the Estanha family was considerably less prestigious than the Tsanaras.

"What I'm trying to *say*," Kira rallied, "is that maybe it's less about you, or even about AUTDRI's budget, and more that he's annoyed he has to rely on a Tsanara to get the whole thing off the ground."

Ellie mulled the idea as she sipped her tea, and hoped that Kira was wrong. The very last thing this project needed was even *more* politics.

4

"So how did things go with the indispensable Stella Hartford?" Liam slipped into his seat, sliding her a full coffee mug as he did. She took a deep, vitalizing sip before answering.

"Probably as good as they were going to. The intro was a little rough but once I got her talking it was a very productive session."

He raised his eyebrows. "Rough intro? To you? What happened?"

Ellie shrugged and took another sip of coffee. "The usual. She wanted you, not me. But after I explained that cooperating with me would lead to getting a visit from you - not in those words, but basically that - she settled down."

"Joke's on her, you're the interesting one. I just talk about math."

"But you're the one who can send her back in time. And you know, I'm still not entirely sure what the deal is with that."

Liam turned in his seat to regard her. "You say that like something weird happened."

"Not...weird, exactly." Even now she struggled to put the

feeling of something being slightly *off* into words. "It just felt like…like there was a piece missing, if that makes sense. When we talked about the Planetary Address, she was very matter of fact about the whole thing, like the conversation was a checklist to get through. Don't get me wrong, her detail recall was amazing, she just…didn't seem as personal about it, as she did some of the other memories we discussed.

"And yeah, she wanted to talk to you and not me, but even then, she didn't seem that interested in…" Ellie wiggled her fingers and dropped her voice to finish in a stage whisper. "*Chronomancy.*" Liam rolled his eyes good-naturedly.

"Well, I can't see what she wants from me then, if it's not *that.*"

"That's kind of the thing. It felt like…like going back was her big goal, and dealing with us was the boxes she had to check to get there, but at the same time she didn't seem all that *excited* about going back. It was just weird."

Liam shrugged. "Unexpected, sure. But as long as we're getting what we need to make the jump, it's her own business why she wants to come, right? And it's working out pretty well for us, too. Career-making project, right out of grad school?" He clinked her mug. "I'm not going to argue."

"Me neither," she admitted. "And you're right, ultimately it doesn't matter so long as we can make the jump as planned." It didn't, but the feeling persisted that she was missing something important. Hopefully it was just anxiety about the project in general.

"How's it going, field team?" Dahlia swept over to their desk looking far too chipper for first thing in the morning. "Can't wait for the full report on what we got from Stella. From what you said yesterday, it sounds like it was a fruitful visit?"

Ellie gave them the overview of what she'd discussed with Stella, including the possibility of their second jump being the Last Landing. From the way Liam's eyes lit up at the idea, it was probably almost guaranteed.

But first things first: they had a preliminary jump to plan.

"So we know that we want a lower-stakes target for the first jump, and also one that's not quite as far back as the Landing itself - but still far back enough to be academically interesting. When I asked Stella about memories of her early life on Altren that most stood out to her, she had a few that seemed promising for a jump."

Ellie grabbed a pad of paper and started writing in big letters. "The first was an incident at Altren University when she was a student, seventy-two years ago." She pinned the page that said *University Class, 4005* to the board, then turned to face her audience. "We'd be jumping to a history course about Plenisar during and after the Altren Migration, in spring 4005."

Liam's brow creased. "She was taking a course on Plenisar during the Migration? Wasn't she *there* for that?"

"She was," Ellie confirmed, "which is what made the whole experience surreal enough that she remembers it in great detail almost seventy-five years later. For the rest of the class, it was ancient history of someplace far away, but for Stella it was the home she'd left just a few years prior."

"I can see how that would stick with you."

"Indeed. For the research interest on that one, we'd get a view of the University roughly twenty years after its founding. So not worldshaking, but also not a jump we'd easily have access to otherwise."

She added her next page to the board: *First Home, 4015.* "Stella bought her first flat about ten years later, after she'd started work as a civil engineer. She had very vivid memories of standing on the balcony looking over the city, letting it sink in that it was *hers* now. This one could be interesting if we're able to wander the building a bit and get a look at daily life for average Altreni. But," she acknowledged, "it has its drawbacks too."

"We'd need cooperation from the current owner, for one," Dahlia commented. "And they may not be enthused about letting us take over their home for a few weeks in the name of science."

"Or," Liam countered, "Maybe they'd be really excited to be a part of the project."

"It's a dice roll," Ellie agreed. She pinned *Building Opening, 4022.*

"The third one was the first ribbon-cutting for one of her buildings. She'd been at the civil engineering firm for several years at that point, but this was the first time she'd led the designs. She remembers intensely how it felt to watch the doors officially open and people go inside something that had started out as a sketch in her notebook. This one's the most recent, only fifty-five years back."

Dahlia chewed her pen. "There's definitely interest there, if it's a building that's still in use. At the same time, we'd need to block off a lot of public space for the jump, which adds complexity and expense."

Liam's lips curved up. "And I'm going to guess our budget doesn't have a *ton* of padding built in?"

"Our budget has *zero* padding built in, and Renton keeps dropping lines about how *great* it would be if we came in under. Every credit we save on this jump is one I can apply towards one of the other two."

"Which are both infinitely more important," Ellie finished for her. "In that case, I'd propose eliminating this last one. I'm sure it's a lovely building, but it's not a landmark, and it's recent enough that there are other people on Altren with memories of that time." She took the page down from the board. "That leaves these two. Any thoughts?"

"What's your recommendation, Ellie? As practical historian?"

"The first one." She didn't even have to think about it. "It takes place on University property, so we don't have to worry about securing the venue. It also shouldn't cost too much to prepare." Anything they could do to bring Stella's memory close to the surface, to evoke the feelings of *being there,* would help strengthen the sync needed to open the portal. Ellie couldn't help a rueful chuckle. "I don't think the humanities part of campus has *ever* been remodeled. We can probably use the very same classroom Stella did, and that alone might be enough to get us there on the nostalgia."

"It's not like you need a new building to understand books," Dahlia agreed cheerfully.

"Besides just the practicalities," Ellie added, "it's far back enough that we won't get many more chances to visit that time-frame. University life in the early 4000s is a bit niche, but it's still an important part of Altren's history. I don't think we'd be sacrificing academic value for budget."

Liam leaned back. "Well, you've convinced me. I vote the University jump, for all the reasons you just said, and also because the entire campus is less than a kilometer across , so well within the safe zone. We'll be able to see pretty much anything at the University without getting far enough away to risk the stability of the time portal."

Dahlia clapped her hands. "Sounds like that's settled then. Can you be ready to go in two weeks?"

Oh suns, that was not a lot of time.

"We pretty much *have* to be to make the rest of the timeline, don't we?" Liam's tone was breezy, but from the look in his eyes he was thinking the same thing as Ellie. "We'll have it done."

"*Great.*" Dahlia swept up her pile of notebooks and headed towards the door, possibly aiming to be through it before they could reconsider. "I'll have the project timeline over to you both later today."

A flutter of nervous excitement ran through her. It was official now, and the clock was on.

———

18:00 sharp at the end of the week meant two things in Ellie's house. First, it was the appointed time for her standing weekly call with her parents. Secondly, and as a result, it was the cleanest her little apartment would be all week.

Ellie finished drying the last of the week's dishes and stowed them away, taking care to get the balance *just right* so that the cabinet would actually close. The speed at which dirty dishes piled up always took her by surprise, it didn't feel like she was even *home* enough to generate that many dishes. But then, when your apartment's sole kitchen counter surface was a half-meter wide, a week's worth of coffee cups took over the space fast.

It would be less work if she sat facing the kitchen for the call, instead of facing the door with the kitchen behind her, but the kitchen had a window that made the space look slightly bigger. Particularly with her bed folded carefully into the wall, so she could pretend that she lived in an apartment with more than one room.

It was a bit silly of her, but…her parents were so *proud* of her, everyone in West Ag 3 seemed to be. The only one in her year to qualify for University, now living a glamorous life in Altren City with an advanced degree and a prestigious research job. She didn't have the heart to tell them that she could barely afford these four walls, she lived off instant protein meals when she wasn't at work, and the existence of the work itself was rather precarious. She didn't *lie*, not outright, but there was no harm in maintaining the illusion things were going better, right?

Of course, that illusion would only hold until someday when her parents came to actually visit, but if things worked out at AUTDRI maybe she'd be able to move somewhere with a door between the kitchen and the bedroom before then. Assuming they could keep AUTDRI afloat long enough for her to get a raise.

She resolutely set the line of thinking aside. Happy thoughts. Everything going well. New job was great and she definitely hadn't been threatened by the head of the University. Smile.

She settled her handheld in front of her and clicked to connect to the West Ag 3 Public Terminal. Several long seconds later, the screen resolved into a grainy image of her parents seated inside one of the Terminal's call booths.

Her smile turned genuine, and a little bittersweet. She really did miss her family terribly, even if she didn't mean to ever move back to the Agsteads.

"It's Altren University's newest top researcher!" Her dad's grin lit up the whole screen, even through the low quality of the feed. "It's so good to see you, Ellie, we've been thinking about you all week!"

Her mom leaned closer to the camera. "Did your first week go well?"

"It went great," Ellie lied. "Everyone at AUTDRI has been really welcoming, and we're already starting on a really big project." Mostly not a lie this time: technically, the Chancellor was not part of AUTDRI.

"That's wonderful! Tell us everything."

She told them a carefully edited version of everything.

"*Plenisar?* That's incredible, Ellie. And for your first project, too." Her mom's brows furrowed slightly. "I'm surprised they started you off with something that complex."

"They knew they needed the best on the job," Ellie's dad answered for her. "We're so proud of you, sweetheart."

She smiled back, though it hit a bit too close to the parts of the story she was trying to avoid. *The chancellor doesn't think I'm the best, but also maybe he just doesn't like AUTDRI in general, or maybe actually he just doesn't like Liam's family, and if this turns into a big-family political game I just hope I don't get squished by it* was not the sort of response her parents needed to deal with.

Instead, she went for a subject change. "How was *your* week? It's about time to get the spring wheat planted, isn't it?"

Her parents exchanged looks briefly. "It's going all right." Her dad's tone was unconvincing. "The wheat planting is a little behind schedule this year, we'd hoped to finish this week but it looks like it's going to take a bit longer. One of the seeder droids went out, so we're having to do more by hand than we'd planned to. It'll be fine though, we'll get it all done in the planting window."

"West Ag 3 lost another seeder?" Ellie couldn't keep the alarm out of her voice. "Are they going to repair it?"

Another brief exchange of glances. "Not this time," her mom answered. "Peron said the main circuit board went out, and there's worn-out spots he can't fix. The rest of it was still in working order, though," she added quickly, "so it's not a total loss. The parts from this one will help make sure we can repair the others when they need it."

None of them said the obvious but it loomed nonetheless in the quiet. *Until the circuit boards go out on those too.*

"It's fine though," her mom assured her. "Like your dad said, we'll still make the planting window just fine. Just a little bit more elbow grease this year is all."

It wasn't fine at all, but if her parents wanted to pretend that all was well in West Ag 3 then Ellie would pretend along with them. It wouldn't change the reality: the majority of the Agsteads' heavy labor was done by the big farm droids, and those droids were slowly breaking down.

When Ellie was a girl, West Ag 3's Chief Technician Peron had seemed like a miracle worker, resurrecting a droid every time it went offline. She knew more about electronics now, of course, understood that hardware degraded over time and sometimes it was simply too far gone to fix. Hearing that the latest breakdown had been beyond his abilities still felt like a pillar of her world had cracked.

Unless the Materials researchers finally found a way to synthesize those critical minerals that Altren lacked, farming was going to become a lot more manual over the next decades. What that meant for the Agsteads - and Altren City that depended on them for food - she wasn't sure she wanted to think about.

So instead she told them more about the preparations they were making for the first jump, and her concerns about the project timelines, and the intriguing things she'd heard from Stella in their initial meetings, and let the shadow of the uncertain future recede back out of sight.

5

The morning of the jump there was a small crowd gathered outside the humanities building. Apparently, word had gotten out that AUTDRI was conducting their first real field mission, and half the university wanted to witness it. Not that they really *could*, the jump was taking place indoors, but plenty of people had shown up anyway.

Ellie couldn't blame them for being excited. Compared to the ultimate goal of the project, today's jump wasn't terribly significant, but it was a big step forward for Altren. She and Liam had made time jumps in their graduate work, of course - their entire thesis project had been time jumps. But this would be the furthest they'd ever traveled back in time, which meant it was the furthest back *anyone* on Altren had traveled back in time.

It was a record that would only stand a few weeks, until their next jump further in Stella's memory, but it was still a significant moment. No one was saying it aloud, but today's jump was proof AUTDRI finally had a reason to exist...and proof that Altren scientists could keep up with Plenisar. They were jumping seventy-two years today; the furthest jump yet made on Plenisar was seventy-nine.

And so Ellie couldn't blame the crowd for being excited. She *could* blame them for blocking her access to the building. She was forced to use her elbows more than once as she squeezed through the thick knot of people, and tried not to grouse to herself that they'd probably moved aside for *Liam*.

Whispers picked up behind her as she finally cleared the ring of onlookers and flashed her ID to the security guard posted by the door. He held it open for her with a smile and a "Good morning, Dr. Nelseren." More whispers, and a spark of smug satisfaction Ellie wasn't especially proud of. *That's right everyone, there's more people working on this project than the "chronomancer."*

Plenty of those other people were running around inside. Grad students were setting up various bits of equipment - surreal, that had been her and Liam just a few months ago - and there were last-minute calculations being scribbled out on the boards. Dahlia was directing several of their assistants through some kind of set preparation; she waved at Ellie and pointed upstairs. Ellie nodded her thanks and headed up.

In the upstairs classroom where Stella had sat nearly three-quarters of a century earlier, she finally found Liam himself. He was occupied exactly as she'd expected: bent over the distortion generator, carefully tuning one of its parameters. He looked up and smiled as she joined him.

"You ready to make history? For a month or two at least," he added, dark eyes gleaming, "before we go and make history again."

Ellie took up a spot leaning against a nearby desk. "It's weird to think about, actually. Under other circumstances, today's jump would actually be pretty significant. Seventy-two years back. There aren't many people who remember that, even fewer who would remember being at the University. Altren was barely even *Altren* then, the last colony ship had only landed five years earlier. When you think about it like *that*, we should be buzzing about what an amazing paper this will make."

Liam joined her in leaning against the desk. "But since we're going to *real actual Plenisar* before all this is over, it feels like a warmup. Which, I guess it is." His lips quirked. "We're coming up in the world, Ellie. Before you know it, researchers on Plenisar will be citing *us*."

A sharp rap on the half-ajar door startled her before she could respond. Dahlia leaned into view. "Anything sensitive you still need to calibrate, or can I send in the interns to set up? We're expecting Stella in the next half-hour."

"We're good on calibrations," Liam confirmed. Ellie nodded her agreement.

"Send them in. Let's make sure we're ready to go when the guest of honor arrives."

———

The room went silent in anticipation as Liam tapped in the sequence. Closest to them was Stella herself, brow furrowed, focused as they'd instructed her on the memory of being in this place. Further back the rest of the AUTDRI team watched raptly, the interns crowded in behind Dahlia and the other physicists. Even Chancellor Felden had made an appearance, lips pressed in a hard line as he watched them prepare to jump. Ellie was proud she hadn't reacted to Liam's murmured joke about performance anxiety, pitched for her ears alone.

He was all professional poise, now. A few more taps, a quick flick of a dial, and the air before them blurred and sparked blue. The blue coalesced into a solid, softly-glowing circle, large enough to enter. The generator *pinged* its satisfaction; the portal was stable and ready to use. Liam gave the room behind them a brief wave of acknowledgment, then took Ellie's hand and stepped them through.

She'd never quite gotten used to the sensation of the time portals. It was something between passing through a thin veil, and being splashed from an ephemeral waterfall. As always, the feeling was over almost as soon as she registered it, and they were standing in the past.

The tableau was still frozen - they'd have a few minutes before they were fully synced with the world of the past, and able to observe as life unfolded around them. For now, they could just take in the scenery.

The classroom itself did look much the same, especially with the set pieces Dahlia had procured. She'd done a good job on the vintage posters, and the ones the interns had put up an hour ago in their own time wouldn't be out of place here alongside the real thing. The biggest difference, of course, was that *this* classroom was in use.

The neat lines of desks were almost fully occupied by students, watching with varying levels of interest as the professor gestured from the board. With a start, Ellie recognized twenty-year-old Stella at a desk near the room's midpoint, fingers frozen over her personal computer. Almost as startling was that *everyone* had a personal computer, as if they were not too precious to entrust to undergrads.

Liam released her hand and glanced around; he'd zeroed in on the same thing. "Did they not realize we were going to run out of these?"

Ellie had her notebook open already, furiously scribbling. "It must not have seemed real then. They were still close enough to the Arrival that they had plenty of supplies."

"Yes, I guess the electronics die-off seemed like a problem for *our* generation, not theirs." He glanced around, then back at the generator console in his hands. "We should get wherever we want to watch from, we're about to finish syncing."

Ellie hurried them over to a corner of the room. She and Liam would be invisible to anyone they encountered, naturally - the distortions allowed one to visit the past, not to interact with it. But she did want an unobstructed view of Stella and the class, for whatever was about to happen next that was memorable enough for Stella to recall decades later in great detail. She readied her notebook; thirty seconds later, the room abruptly came to life. Keyboards tapped, students fidgeted, the professor picked up mid-lecture.

"And keep in mind, it wasn't just those large natural disasters - although those large disasters were coming closer and closer together, were becoming almost a part of the fabric of daily life. But there was also just the everyday background degradation of the human habitat.

"Crop yields were affected by the soil issues and the more extreme weather conditions, and we know from contemporary media and personal writing that this seriously impacted people's diets. Air quality was measurably worse than it had been a few decades earlier. A child born in the late 3700s was more likely than their grandparents to suffer from respiratory conditions, and a shorter life expectancy overall, simply because the air they were breathing was so much unhealthier."

He turned to look at the class. "I was nine years old when we left Plenisar on the first colony ship, and I don't remember much about it, but I *do* remember my first breath on Altren. It was the first actually clean air I'd tasted in my life. And these conditions were *global*, by that time," he added. "There was nowhere on Plenisar that wasn't affected."

The professor gestured again at the board, where these problems and more were listed in neat bullets. "And so you can see why, by the turn of the century, Plenisar's ability to continue to sustain life was in serious doubt. So much so that establishing *the first human colony in space* seemed like a better solution than trying to salvage it."

He turned to face the class more fully. "Let that sink in for a moment. Humanity had made such a mess of our home planet, we didn't think it was possible to fix. The Altren Migration was an act of desperation. The terraforming project was a huge success, obviously, and it's easy to lose sight of just how *bad* things were before then. But back when terraforming was just starting up, in many ways the odds seemed impossible. Maria Hartford gets credit for leading the science on the project, and she did, but what she *also* did was give people hope that saving Plenisar was possible."

His eyes rested on Stella, whose hands had gone still above her keyboard.

"I know this is ancient history for most of you," he went on. "Of the people in this room, how many were born here on Altren?"

All but Stella raised their hands. The professor nodded.

"When I first started teaching, most of my classes were Plenisari transplants, just like me. But every year there's fewer, and not that far in the future we'll just be notes in your history books." His smile was wry. "I'm likely to be the last one teaching this class who was *actually* there. But this year we do have a fellow Plenisari with us, and not just anyone."

He nodded genially at Stella, apparently oblivious to how she'd tensed under the words. "Stella, Maria Hartford was actually your sister, wasn't she?"

The room turned as one to look at her. If she had been watching Stella less carefully, Ellie might have missed her tiny wince at *was*.

"Yes." Stella's voice was quiet, though it was unclear whether her obvious discomfort stemmed from the subject or the sudden stares of everyone in the room. "I'm Maria's little sister."

"What was she like?"

"She was...very determined. And brave. And very smart. It was..." Stella paused, her words taking on a practiced cadence. "It was an honor to be her sister, and we're very proud of everything she accomplished for humanity."

She was saved from any further questions by the chimes signaling the top of the hour - and apparently the end of the class period. Almost before the ringing ceased, Stella had gathered her things and darted out of the room.

"Well, that was awkward." Liam's gaze lingered on the door she'd exited. "Do you think that happened a lot?"

"Hard to say. Judging by her reaction she didn't like to talk about it."

"Especially since the fact that Stella's *here* means Maria's own family didn't believe terraforming was going to work. She rallied Plenisar while they got on the last ship to Altren. I wouldn't be surprised if there's some complicated feelings there."

Ellie mulled that for a moment. Even with her parents' unflagging support, she felt badly sometimes for leaving them and the rest of her family behind in the Agsteads, to chase a better future at the University. And they were only a call away. What would it be like, to know you left your sister behind forever?

Her gaze lingered on where Stella had sat. "I wonder if *complicated feelings* are related to why we're here in the first place."

Liam tapped a key on the console. "Regardless of *why* Stella came to the lab today, we've still got almost two hours until she's supposed to go home. I'm guessing we have everything we need from right here?"

It was a rhetorical question; the classroom had emptied of everyone but the professor, unhurriedly erasing the board for the next class. Ellie nodded her agreement anyway.

"We should use the remaining time to get out to the rest of campus, yes. You said we can make it to the science buildings?"

"Easily. As long as we don't leave the university grounds, we'll stay well within the safe zone." He gestured affectionately at their only path home, its faint blue glow visible only to them. "The hole in time and space will be right here when we get back."

"Well then." She slipped her notebook into her bag and hiked it into a more comfortable position. "Let's go for a walk."

———

The most striking thing about the Altren University of 4005 was how much it *hadn't* changed. There were minor differences, of course - an odd configuration of benches, an unfamiliar land-scaping feature, a missing building wing - but on the whole it still felt familiar. The same suns shone overhead with gentle spring warmth, the same swirl of students populated the campus around them. The fashions on those students might be slightly different than the present day, but Ellie still wouldn't blink if they were dropped into modern Altren.

The buildings themselves had changed even less, at least here in the humanities sector. They were significantly less weathered, and some were a different color. The occasional coat of paint seemed to be the extent of the attention they'd received over the years.

It was a bit irritating, to be visibly reminded that the University didn't think your field was worth investing resources in, but at the same time she understood. Dahlia was right, after all - you didn't need a new building to study books.

Familiar as the humanities sector might be, she still pulled out her notebook to take down what notes she could. A recording device would have been more efficient, naturally. But whatever way time and space folded to allow them to visit the past, it prevented mechanical recording as well; no one had ever managed to get anything but white noise. Several labs on Plenisar were actively trying to develop distortion-compatible recording tech, but the results they'd published so far didn't seem particularly promising. Like the "chronomancers," recording media within a distortion was a mystery that seemed unlikely to be answered anytime soon.

Even if it was, Altren probably wouldn't have the materials to solve for it anyway. Ellie had gotten quite practiced at scrib-bling notes while she walked.

She took down as much detail as she could on everything they passed. None of this was *groundbreaking*, of course. It was all recent enough that there was a plethora of extant records on what people wore and ate, and Altren itself was too new for society to have changed that much since the Founding. But here and there they still saw hints of a different world - much like they'd noticed in Stella's classroom.

"*Everyone* has electronics," Liam murmured. "*Everyone.*" And they did. Personal computing devices of various sizes and shapes dotted the crowds around them, as if it were perfectly commonplace for everyone to have one. Ellie found herself wondering if that was true outside the University - or even the city. If they'd been able to travel from here to the Agsteads, would the farmers there have computers in their pockets just like these? Would there be no need for the public terminals?

"Do you think they were issued by the University," she mused aloud, "or do they just…have them?"

"Could be hand-me-downs, if their parents took care of theirs." He said it off-handedly, as if personal electronics were something most families might reasonably own and hand down. If you were a Tsanara, maybe most families you knew *did*.

Liam glanced over quickly; maybe some of her thoughts had shown on her face. "We're still pretty close to the Last Landing," he pointed out. "And personal tech was a lot more common on Plenisar. Whatever people brought with them could still be in working order."

"True." She eyed a student at one of the nearby tables as the young woman set down her handheld and turned to talk to a friend. "Hang on, I want a sketch of that."

It never stopped feeling weird, and a bit creepy, to walk right up to someone and stand there undetected as they went about their business. Nevertheless, Ellie sidled up to the group of oblivious students, a ghost in their distant past, and quickly sketched out the details of the device on the table. She put particular effort into capturing the logo imprinted under the screen; with luck, there would be information in the Archives about where it came from.

Liam was accustomed Ellie's sudden stops on these trips, and waited patiently until she had what she needed - and twice more, when they passed unattended devices on their way. Finally, they crossed over into the part of campus dedicated to studying the sciences, and for the first time stepped into unfamiliar territory.

Ellie might not have recognized it, if she didn't know where she was. The placement of the buildings was roughly the same, but the structures themselves had undergone significant refitting in the last seventy-odd years. Different paint, different exterior siding, different configurations of doors and windows, indicating most had undergone at least *some* expansion.

The most dramatic difference from the present day was the Material Science hall. Here, it was almost indistinguishable from the chemistry and biology halls that flanked it. The entire structure was only about a third of its current size, missing a large wing *and* its entire second story. If building size indicated a department's value, it seemed Altren in 4005 hadn't quite realized that it lacked the raw materials to replicate the technology brought from Plenisar, and that all these omnipresent electronics had a shelf life.

"Let's do a walk-around of the Materials building and get a sketch in." She started towards it, knowing he'd be right on her heels. "I'm sure there are renovation records buried somewhere in the Archives, but it's interesting to see visible evidence that the University hadn't started to focus on material development yet, even as late as this. I wonder when the shift got underway in earnest."

Liam fell into step next to her. "It's been a few decades at least. A few decades of almost exclusive funding," he added with a touch of disgruntlement, "and Materials *still* hasn't managed to deliver any real progress on synthesizing a replacement for what we're missing. Who knows, maybe if they'd started earlier they just would have wasted even *more* money."

There was a venomous undercurrent to that last bit, that sounded a bit deeper than just professional annoyance at competing with Materials for budget. She made an educated guess.

"Are your parents on you again?"

He grimaced. "I had dinner over there a few nights ago. Got the 'why don't you do something useful for Altren' speech over dessert."

"Still?" She didn't look up, concentrating on capturing the odd swoop in the roof's corner. It looked vaguely familiar; she wondered if that section of the building had been repurposed elsewhere in Altren City after a remodel.

"Still. It's like, Mom, I'm literally the only one on Altren who can move this field forward, I *just* finished grad school, and you want me to go back and start over again in the planet's most saturated field. I'm not sure what they think *I'm* going to be able to do that everyone *currently* researching materials can't."

He laughed a little, the annoyance in his voice dissipating. "Though listening to Renton, sometimes I think it's going to be an even bigger challenge to keep AUTDRI open long enough to get any real data. Speaking of," he added, examining the console's readings, "We should start walking back pretty soon if we're going to finish on time."

"Wouldn't do to keep Stella waiting around past the schedule," she agreed. "Not before we've even gotten to the good stuff. I can be done here in just a sec."

They finished the walkaround for completeness' sake, and Ellie managed to get in one more quick sketch of an outdoor lab before they headed back to the humanities buildings. As expected, the portal was where they'd left it, though now it sat in the midst of a class on Plenisar's industrialization. As curious as she was about that - was it taught with a different lens, so close to the Migration, than it was when she'd taken it a century later? - they were indeed out of time, and she could only catch a few words as Liam took her hand and stepped them through the glowing blue.

The strange sensation of passing through the portal and then they were back, standing in the same classroom in the present day. The room was still packed, even after two hours, and an eager buzz started up almost immediately. There was even a smattering of applause, which seemed a bit absurd - *you'd think we'd never done this before* - but she'd take it. Even Felden, glowering from the back of the room, gave them a small nod before turning to leave.

This jump may have been minor for historical significance, but it had gone exactly to plan. They had their first win at the department.

6

f the first jump had come up quickly, the second one hurtled towards them with all the velocity of a meteor. There was hardly time to celebrate their success before it was time to shift focus to what came next.

Part of Ellie had hoped that with the success of the first jump, the second would be less nerve-racking. After all, they'd proven now that they could do it: Stella's memories were viable, and Liam had successfully navigated one of the furthest time jumps ever recorded. On their first try, even. There was no reason to be anxious about doing it again.

Except that the first jump, for all its impressive metrics, was ultimately inconsequential. Their few hours observing the University and its students was interesting from a social history perspective, certainly, but too narrow a window to draw any significant conclusions. And even the University would have to admit that its history was unlikely to be of interest to anyone outside, well, the University.

The Last Landing, on the other hand, was of interest to *everyone*.

No one involved in the Last Landing had *expected* it to be the last, when they set out. Dozens of colony ships had launched from Plenisar in those chaotic, dangerous decades, eager to leave behind the dying planet for a new future on Altren. The expectation had been that ships would continue to launch, until the last dregs of Plenisar's resources were exhausted, and "everyone who could be saved, had been."

That was how it was described in the official records, anyway. The phrase had always given Ellie a bit of a chill. Unspoken in it was the understanding that most of humanity could *not* be saved, that the millions whose merit or influence had secured them a seat to Altren were leaving behind billions to suffocate and starve. That if her great-great-grandmother had not pulled a winning ticket in the lottery for the limited "social equity" seats reserved for the working class, her family would never have been deemed worthy to survive.

Ellie shook off the dark feeling. The moment they would jump to was significant precisely *because* things had not turned out so bleak after all. The reason there were no other colony ships landing after this one was not because Plenisar had died afterwards, but because it had been saved.

Dahlia's arrival cut off any further ruminating. They were visiting the Archives today, to find what information they could on what the spaceport had been like back when it had been operational. With no more ships arriving from Plenisar, and neither the capability nor the clear need to manufacture their own spacecraft, Altren's only spaceport was defunct in all but name. Ellie privately suspected that it hadn't yet been repurposed for parts only because tearing it down was a statement Altren City wasn't quite ready to make.

"Good morning!" In the bright early sunlight, the red streaks in Dahlia's hair seemed even more vivid. "The suns are out, the birds are singing...ready to go spend all day in a windowless room underground?"

Ellie couldn't help her giggle. "You know it. Though when

you put it like *that* it makes me wonder what I'm doing with my life."

"Right there with you," her project manager agreed. "The University's basement is definitely not where I thought *I'd* end up either, but duty calls."

Come to think of it, Ellie was rather curious about that. "How *did* you end up at AUTDRI, Dahlia?"

She shrugged. "Luck? Weird life choices? I kind of fell into it, honestly. I studied theatre."

"Really? Theatre?"

"Really, theatre. Mostly backstage management, I'm a decent actress but I never wanted to make a career out of it. But there's not a lot of theatre job openings in general," she laughed, though with an undercurrent of bitterness, "and even fewer that actually pay money."

Ellie nodded sympathetically. "I imagine the arts funding is not terribly good right now."

"If it ever was. But yeah, same story everywhere, all the budget is getting sucked into dealing with the electronics crisis. The Altren City Repertory still gets funded, but the city gives less grant money every year, and with jobs at the ACR you pretty much have to wait for the person currently doing them to die. So I needed to find something else."

"And something else was AUTDRI?"

Dahlia's short hair swished with her nod. "One of my set-design professors recommended me. I've always been good at running group projects, and it turns out creating the environment for these jumps is not so far off from a theatre set. It's all about that convincing illusion. Speaking of?" She gestured for Ellie to go ahead of her, and together they descended into the Archives.

The chill set in immediately as soon as they cleared the first flight of stairs. Spring might be rapidly warming the days outside, but it was always winter in the Archives. Some of the most valuable computing resources still functional on Altren were housed here.

Ellie had never actually *seen* one of the Archive's primary servers, of course. The University might be devoting a great deal of time and money to dedigitizing its records, but it was still an enormous project. And until the work was completed, vast swathes of information were an error away from vanishing. Only highly-trained Archivists were allowed anywhere near the servers themselves.

But with hardware failure an arguably bigger threat, the entire floor was aggressively cooled to prevent any of those irreplaceable resources from overheating. Even the rooms for the dedigitized records, with their rows and rows of manuscript boxes filled to the brim with crisp paper records, were kept at a low temperature to aid preservation. You could always tell who was visiting the Archives for the first time - they were the ones shivering without jackets.

Ellie, on the other hand, was snug in her fleece-lined coat. She noted with interest that Dahlia had come prepared as well - despite AUTDRI's limited fieldwork, it wasn't her first time down here either.

The thought was confirmed when they were greeted at the front desk with equal familiarity. Fortunately the Archives weren't busy, and so they hardly had to wait at all before an Archivist was available to assist them. She broke out in a grin when she saw who it was.

Matheus one of the more popular Archivists, for good reason. While some of his colleagues could be a bit stuffy, she'd never seen him with anything less than overflowing enthusiasm for helping people find information. But there was another reason why Mat was Ellie's favorite. He was an Agsteads transplant too, a few years ahead of her from the orchards of East Ag 1.

He greeted them with his usual good cheer. "And what can I do for you both today? Is this official AUTDRI business? Are we cracking open mysteries of space and time?"

"It's AUTDRI business," she confirmed with a smile. "But no mysteries of time today. Maybe next week."

"We're looking for anything you have on when the spaceport was functional." Dahlia was already pulling a list out of her bag. "Particularly around the time of the Last Landing. Layouts, usage patterns, vessel landing configurations...I'll even take the interior design, if you've got it. Contemporary accounts preferred."

Matheus scanned down the list. "We've got at least some of this, for sure. I can get you started with the blueprints for the landing pads and the flight protocols sent to the terminal. And I think the inventories from the *Peregrine*'s cargo are already dedigitized, so I can have copies made of those for you to take back to the office. Not sure we have anything granular enough to cover the decor, but if we do I'll find it." He looked back at them, eyes wide. "Wait, are you going back to *the Last Landing?*"

"We are." As nervous as she was about all this, Ellie couldn't help a swell of pride. They were doing something big here. "Less than a month from today."

"I'd better get you those docs in a hurry then." He paused on his way back out of the room to glance back at them. "Remember to put me in the article about AUTDRI's breakthroughs in chronomancy, okay?"

Sorry, Liam, Ellie thought ruefully. *I think that one's going to stick.*

———

Liam stretched in his chair, almost knocking his hand into the wall beside their desks. "Well, I think that's as far as I'm getting today. We're in good shape and the rest of this will still be here after the weekend. I think it's time to go home."

Ellie glanced at the clock on the wall with a start. Early afternoon had somehow slid into early evening while she was working through the latest documents Mat had found her. Come to think of it, her back hurt too from hunching over her desk, and it *was* time to go home.

Or somewhere, at least. They'd made it through another week and the jump *was* in good shape. That seemed worth celebrating.

"We could probably still make happy hour at the Corner," she offered. "It's been a while since we've been, the bar staff might forget our names if we don't pop in soon." What the aptly-named Corner Bar lacked in ambiance or fancy drinks, it made up for with friendliness and familiarity. Also, more importantly, it was cheap, even *without* half-off pours. They'd been regular enough in grad school that the staff already knew their orders.

Instead of the answering grin she expected, Liam went suddenly tense, his previous smile wiping off his face. "I can't," he answered, eyes fixed on the desk as though it were suddenly fascinating. "I, uh." He sighed almost imperceptibly. "I have a date."

"Oh." The surprised syllable was out of her mouth before she could think; her mind felt empty of everything but *what?* It was followed immediately by, *well of course.* Liam was brilliant, good-looking, *and* leading a groundbreaking science project. Really, it was more surprising that he was single in the first place. It had just…never really come up.

But it was coming up now, and when your best friend tells you they have a date, you should probably say something better than "oh." She cast around frantically for something less awkward to say, finally settling on a bright, "Congratulations!"

Internal wince, that was not much less awkward. Try again.

"No really, that's great, I'm so happy for you." Better! "I didn't realize you were even seeing anyone." Shit, did that sound weird? She was making it weird, wasn't she.

"I'm not." The answer came quickly, though he didn't lift his gaze. Apparently packing his bag had suddenly become a task that required his full attention. At least he seemed oblivious to Ellie's inner flailing.

"I'm not seeing anyone," he repeated, "not really. There's this one girl my parents have been on me to talk to, I don't even really know her, it's more like our parents are friends. I finally just said yes so they'd get off me about it."

A girl from a good family, then, if her parents were friends with Liam's. Not anyone Ellie would know, naturally; a girl from the kinds of parties Ellie was not invited to. Well, of course it was, *of course* there would be certain standards for the Tsanara scion's prospective partners.

She realized she'd gone silent again, which wasn't helping the sudden awkwardness that had settled over the table like a stifling blanket. "Um…well, I hope you have more fun than you're expecting, then?"

He finally glanced up at her, a faint spark of amusement in his dark eyes. "Thanks. The bar's pretty low there, in any case."

Her bag was packed and ready to go, and there was really no reason to stay. So she didn't. "I guess I'll see you at the start of the week then. Have a good time." She waved and started out of the room.

"Thanks. And…Ellie?" She paused and glanced back. He was watching her with an odd expression. "Maybe we can hit the Corner next week, yeah?"

Suns, the last thing she needed was for Liam to think she expected some sort of apology for his having a life outside of her. Ellie shrugged, careful to keep her voice light. "Sure, if we feel like it next week. No big deal if not."

She was through the door before he could respond.

———

Ellie was determined to put the whole thing out of her mind and enjoy her own weekend, but the strange conversation continued to hover around her head like one of the winged parasite insects that made summer evenings miserable in the Agsteads. The memory was laced with an odd feeling of hurt, because…what? Because he didn't tell her there was a girl he was maybe, maybe-not seeing? It really wasn't any of her business. Was that it, then, that Liam was her closest friend, and she thought she was his, but it wasn't any of her business? Had there been others he'd just never mentioned? Maybe there was a whole side of Liam's life he'd just never talked about to her.

But no, that seemed unlikely. With how much of the last few years he'd spent with Ellie, working or studying or spending late nights at the Corner, when would he have had *time*?

No…probably, it was exactly what he'd said. She *did* know Liam, and she knew he was absolute trash at talking about things that made him uncomfortable. He probably wouldn't have brought up that his parents were pushing him into dating a girl he barely knew, or that he'd buckled under pressure and agreed.

Certainly, he didn't sound terribly enthused about the whole thing, but maybe it would turn out to be less of a chore than he implied. And while he'd said he was going so they'd "get off him about it," they were unlikely to back off after a single date. Suns above, why was she even still thinking about this?

The buzz of her handheld had never been more welcome.

>Ellie: drinks & DoubleStar in an hour? Just me, Shana already busy. -K

She banged off a fast affirmative response that Kira would hopefully see before leaving her building's comms terminal, and resolved for the millionth time to stop thinking about this stupid thing that was none of her business anyway. A night out was just what she needed.

———

An hour or so later, the evening was already looking up. She was wedged into a booth at DoubleStar, a lightly spiked tea drink in front of her and a big bowl of noodles on the way.

"So, no Shana tonight?"

Kira shook her head. "She had plans with Calla, so. It's just us single ladies tonight."

Hm. "So things with Dan...?"

Kira made a face. "There's no 'things with Dan.' We're done. For real this time."

They almost certainly weren't, Kira and Danell had been doing some version of this on-and-off dance since undergrad, but Ellie knew better than to argue. Who knew, maybe this would be the time one of them finally decided they didn't want to do this anymore. Until then, as Shana was fond of saying, Kira would have to reach that decision her own.

"I was actually surprised *you* were free Ellie, I figured either you'd be working late or you'd be somewhere with Liam celebrating *not* working late."

"I guess this project *has* been taking up most of my time lately." Ellie made a mental note to be more proactive about reaching out to her friends, even when - especially when? - things were busy. "And ah...Liam had a date tonight too, actually. So single ladies it is! How's your work been going lately?" She tried for a carefree smile, hoping her weak attempt at distraction would work.

It didn't. "Wait, *what*?" Kira's eyebrows rose all the way up, tinged with a faint shadow of outrage. "With *who?*"

"I'm not sure, nobody I would know. He said his parents set it up."

"Ohh." Kira relaxed slightly. "Not real, then." Her lips quirked at Ellie's expression. "Society parents do that sometimes, it's annoying. That's why I had dinner with Rolan Martelen that one time, remember? It wasn't *really* a date."

"It might have been real to Rolan," Ellie observed drily.

Kira rolled her eyes and shrugged. "I'm saying there's a difference between checking a box on something so you have leverage to get your parents off your back, and actually giving it a real go." She leaned forward. "Seriously. I'll find out who she is, but you have nothing to worry about as far as whatever's going on with you and Liam."

Kira paused, cocking an assessing glance across the table. "So…what *is* going on with you and Liam?"

Ellie shifted, suddenly feeling defensive. "We're *friends*, Kira. Friends who *work* together, now," she added for good measure.

"Uh-huh. You've been *friends* since undergrad, and in that time you have dated…" she pretended to add up in her head. "*Zero* people."

"That's not true! There was…that one, our third year."

"Mmhm." Kira's expression was irritatingly knowing. "And how did that go?"

Terribly. Ellie had said yes when the guy from her lit class had asked, mainly because she'd been too surprised to say anything else. She'd then spent a stiflingly dull evening picking at her dinner while making painfully awkward small talk with the stranger across the table, and trying not to think about how she could be doing *literally anything else right now.*

There hadn't been a second date.

"Look," Ellie finally managed. "It just caught me off guard tonight, that's all. And…" suns, this was embarrassing to say out loud, "I guess part of me worries that if my best friend gets a girlfriend, he won't have time to spend with me anymore, and I'd miss that. A lot." She knew she must be bright red; it certainly *felt* like her cheeks might burst into flame.

"Mm." From her expression, Kira had a lot of thoughts about that statement, but for once in her life decided not to share them. "I'm pretty sure that's not going to happen, but I guess time will tell. For now, subject change?" She grinned at the open relief on Ellie's expression. "So there was actually a ton of drama in my office this week…"

———

Ellie was the first one in to the AUTDRI office at week-start, and she was just settling back in to an account of the final supplies shipped from Plenisar when the Sunrise Bread logo suddenly dropped into her vision, attached to a paper bag that smelled *incredible*.

"Fresh out of the oven," Liam announced cheerfully, "or at least they were half an hour ago."

She picked up the bag, a hint of warmth still lingering on its surface. Her favorite Sunrise sweetbun was tucked within. "Thank you! What's the occasion?"

"Do we need one?" He cocked his head for half a second. "How about, we're almost done with the second jump and nothing has gone horribly wrong yet. That's an occasion, right? I'm deciding it is."

Ellie was momentarily distracted by the sheer bliss of fresh sugary pastries. And yet…

She paused on her second bite. "You're in a good mood today." He only shrugged, smiling. A sneaking suspicion rose in her mind. "Things with the mystery girl go better than you were expecting?"

"Hm? Oh." He looked slightly embarrassed. "She was nice, I guess, but we didn't really have anything to talk about. I think we were both just kind of waiting around until it was okay to go home. The drinks there were pretty good though, we should go sometime."

Score one for Kira, Ellie thought ruefully, but she couldn't deny the flood of relief through her veins.

Liam shrugged, faint blush still dusting his cheeks. "But? Next time my mom tells me I should really spend more time with Fiora Sentaris, we'd be such a great pair if we just got to know each other, I can say I tried and it wasn't there."

A hint of that warm grin tugged at his lips. "And I imagine Fiora's thinking the same thing. Not that my parents are going to give up, but I've bought some time on that particular subject until they can find someone else to shove at me. Which," he added ruefully, "I guess gives them more opportunities to focus on 'why aren't I doing more for Altren,' but can't win them all. Speaking of everything I'm not contributing to Altren, how're you feeling about the next jump?"

She laughed along and pulled out her notes. "Not bad. Mat was able to pull me a few more primary sources, and Dahlia and I are doing the onsite visit later this week…"

7

Matheus came through for them: besides just the technical details of its general layout and official records of the last few ships to land, he'd found a journal of one of the first spaceport managers in a general information drive that had been donated to the University after her death.

The personal details weren't relevant, of course - though Ellie was deeply tempted to keep reading just to learn how things had turned out in her tempestuous relationship with the director of municipal water management - but the late port manager had also included a number of everyday details on her work. Including, even, a dispute over what color the carpets ought to be.

Dahlia muttered something about how she would kill for a picture or three, and scribbled notes furiously nonetheless.

Fortunately for their purposes, besides the controversial carpets, Altren Spaceport had undergone virtually no renovation since its initial assembly in the first wave of automated construction. The landing pad where Stella had stepped into Altren's air for the first time was still accessible, in the same configuration that had welcomed the last colony ship all those decades ago. The biggest environment preparation *this* time would simply be cleanup. With no actual spaceflight to accommodate, the city government had been using the spaceport as a giant storage unit for decades.

Which was not to say that the task would be easy. Standing in the midst of nearly a century's worth of clutter, Ellie almost couldn't imagine what the space must have been like in its heyday. The piled junk and thick coats of dust were too immediate.

Dahlia only pursed her lips. "It's fine, we'll hire people to help, it'll be ready in time. I didn't have that penciled out in the budget but it's for the Last Landing. It'll get approved. As long as what you and Liam bring back outweighs the value of the extra cost, I don't think even Felden will make an issue."

"I'll let Liam know that's our new performance metric." And hopefully Felden agreed that data from one of Altren's defining events was worth some extra credits on a cleaning crew.

———

Whoever Dahlia had hired for cleanup was worth every credit. When the team arrived at the spaceport for the second jump, they found it utterly transformed. The leaning piles of clutter from Ellie's previous visit had vanished, and every surface had been cleaned and polished to a near-shine.

"You could almost launch a new shuttle out of here now," Liam murmured. "When you told me what it looked like last time, I was half afraid we were going to have to spend this morning mopping."

"Me too," she confessed. "I wasn't entirely sure it was *possible* to get it ready in time, even with extra help."

"Mm. I think it was *cleanomancy.* World's full of mysteries, after all."

She elbowed him just as Dahlia herself rounded the corner, and then there was no time for anything but final checks. Twenty minutes later, she was once again hand-in-hand with Liam, as they stepped through the glowing circle suspended in the chill morning air.

———

Altren's horizon was unchanged as they alighted in the past, its twin suns steadily climbing above the thickly forested hills beyond the city. That was where the similarities ended with the scene they had just left, however. In *this* time, the landing pad was crowded full of people, spilling out from an enormous ship.

The colony ship itself almost defied imagination. The photos in the Archives couldn't do justice to its sheer enormity - the ship just kept going, up and up, a massive superstructure built to hold hundreds of thousands of people suspended in cryosleep. Those people would be waking up in shifts now, and awaiting their turn to leave the ship to begin their new lives. If the portal had brought them here, then Stella's group must be about to take their turn.

Speaking of, they needed to locate her, preferably before the sync finished and the frozen crowd roared to life. Ellie got to work scanning the faces around the platforms. Suns, there were so *many* of them.

"Got her," Liam murmured. He tugged Ellie's hand and drew her quickly over to where a teenage Stella paused at the mouth of the great ship. No sooner had they fallen in beside her than the sync finished, and the din of a thousand conversations exploded around them.

The new arrivals whispered and pointed at the landscape, some mix of nervous and excited energy in the crowd. From more than one direction she caught something about how strange the sky and trees were, how *alien*, and she tried to imagine how Altren would look to people who had never seen it before. She failed. Ellie had never seen Plenisar, and had no idea what a sky and trees "ought" to look like.

The Plenisari, she realized with a burst of amusement, were the aliens here.

Liam gave her a questioning look, but before she could explain young Stella started moving.

Ellie and Liam followed her, and the older couple who must have been her parents, as they moved deeper into the spaceport. The Altreni authorities had set up a receiving center in the spaceport's concourse, and long lines of new arrivals wended and curved around the space. Ellie's hands twitched toward her notebook, but no, this was something to explore on the subsequent jump. This time, they needed to stay with Stella.

Their memorist's group was led to a large conference room, with "Welcome to Altren" written out on the display board in cheerful block letters. When they had all taken seats, a smiling, vaguely-familiar-looking woman in a business suit called them to attention.

"Good morning, and welcome one and all. I'm Jena Tsanara, Mayor of Altren City, and it's my pleasure to welcome you to the planet of Altren, and to the year 3999." Liam startled a bit beside her, but said nothing. Now that she was looking for it, Ellie could recognize his nose and cheekbones in Jena's face. *That* was why she'd seemed familiar.

"As you might imagine," Jena was saying, "a great deal has happened since your departure from Plenisar. And I'm happy to say, some of the news is quite wonderful."

Murmurs picked up among the new arrivals. Given the circumstances in which they'd left Plenisar, "wonderful news" was probably the last thing they expected to hear.

"Many of you may have expected that you would arrive to learn that Plenisar had collapsed, and that Altren contains the last of humanity," she continued. "It is my great pleasure to share that this is not the case. You may remember that shortly before your departure, a terraforming project was announced to restore Plenisar's habitability, led by Dr. Maria Hartford." Jena's smile broadened. "It was successful."

The murmurs intensified to a dull roar; Jena lifted her hand for silence again. "The Plenisar of today supports a thriving population of roughly fourteen billion people. Rather than being alone in an empty universe, we on Altren are part of an expanding web of humanity."

Jena moved on to other subjects then, a quick overview of all that had happened on Altren in the 75 years the new arrivals traveled, and the logistics of settling in the newcomers. Stella, Ellie noticed, didn't seem to be listening.

Their memorist stared at her hands, her thoughts seemingly a million miles away. Her whole demeanor had changed with the news that Maria had been successful, that Plenisar had been saved after all. But while the general mood of the room was relief, Stella didn't seem all that reassured. Ellie might have expected her to be excited for Maria's achievement, or proud, even if the feeling was bittersweet. But the closest she could describe the look on Stella's face was grief. Grief, or perhaps a little guilt.

———

They made the jump three more times, before *their* Stella began to get tired. The first run had been reconnaissance and following Stella through her memory, but the subsequent jumps gave them the opportunity to explore more of the world around her.

They traced paths through the bustling spaceport to observe other groups of new arrivals, hovered in the baggage distribution center for glimpses of what the Plenisari brought with them, and on the fourth jump even ventured inside the great colony ship itself. The interior was just as incredible as the view from outside, all metal and glass, too vast for them to see more than just the sliver they could access from the docking bay.

It was still, Ellie realized with a rush of dizziness, the closest she would ever get to space.

They were prepping for the fifth jump when Liam shook his head.

"We're losing the memory sync," he announced, frowning at the device. "Not enough left for a stable portal. We'll have to be good with what we've already got for today."

Ellie nodded her agreement. Four total jumps from one memory in a single session was quite good; most memorists' concentration started to dull after two. And they'd gathered some valuable material from the time that they'd had. Ellie had pages of detailed notes about the intake process and the new-arrival experiences they'd observed, none of which were currently recorded in the Archives. From her view the day had been a success.

The team started in on breakdown around them, and an assistant helped Stella back into her walker. Ellie's eyes lingered on their memorist's back as she moved away. Young Stella's face in the memory stuck with her. It certainly wasn't Ellie's place to tell anyone how to feel, and she could only imagine the complicated feelings that might arise from the situation with Maria. But she couldn't shake the feeling that there was something else in all this too, something Stella wasn't telling them.

She pushed the thought away. The next few weeks leading up to the Plenisar jump would be intense, and she would need to have all her energy focused on the preparations. Liam was right - whatever secrets Stella may or may not be keeping were her own concern.

8

Preparation for the final jump posed an immediate challenge: there was no extant environment to work from. Restoring the spaceport section to its glory days had been a big task, but under all the clutter and grime the location of Stella's memory was still *there*.

This time, they were traveling to a location across the galaxy. They couldn't exactly go to Plenisar to stage the jump. And so, as Dahlia had pronounced with determined cheer, they would just have to bring Plenisar here.

Alas, the Archives didn't have any books about how to throw a fortieth-century-Plenisar themed party on Altren. By the time they were finished here, though, Ellie mused that they might be able to write one themselves.

"Oh! I think we can make this one!" Dahlia, Liam, and Matheus clustered behind her to peer at the century-old cake recipe on her screen. "One of the grains we grow in the Agsteads is really close to the kind of flour it calls for, and it uses honey for sweetener. Everything else is a standard ingredient."

She glanced over at Matheus for confirmation. His parents were beekeepers, honey was more his area than hers. He nodded his agreement. "It might not be 100% authentic, but I bet we can get pretty close on taste and texture."

"I'll take 'pretty close' at this point," Dahlia commented as she scribbled it down. "Big improvement over 'nothing remotely close to this ingredient exists on our planet.'" The Plenisari, as it turned out, had eaten some rather exotic-sounding things. The food portion of their party planning was much harder than any of them had expected. "Are you both good to keep looking on the food while Liam and I start on costumes? I think you're the best equipped for this part."

"Absolutely." Ellie exchanged an amused glance with Mat. In the years she'd lived in Altren City, this was the first time being from the Agsteads had ever been considered a *plus*. From his wry expression, he was thinking the same.

"Well, if the ag experts have it covered on snacks," Liam agreed, "then I guess I need to make sure we look good doing this."

"That's the spirit." Dahlia pointed to one of the other screens. "There's got to be *something* we can use in all these media records. We've only got three weeks to produce anything we find in here, so let's keep it moving."

Ellie dutifully flipped back to recipe collection and resumed her search. A proper party, after all, would need more than cake.

In the end, their faux-Plenisar party did come together. Ellie and Matheus assembled a reasonable-sounding menu, leaning heavily on vegetables grown on both planets. Liam found a treasure trove of celebrity photos and pulled some stunning options for costumes, though Ellie shouldn't have been surprised. She already knew he had excellent taste. Dahlia had even found a top-100 music hits list from the year they were traveling to, and was already elbow-deep in paperwork to borrow an electronic speaker for the event.

The biggest thing left to prepare for was traveling with Stella herself.

———

Sitting in a lab, passively providing the anchor memory for the distortion generator, was quite simple. All the memorist really needed to do was sit and concentrate; Liam and the generator could take it from there. Actually traveling through the distortion *yourself* was a whole different matter. The only sensation stranger than the feeling of stepping into the portal to visit another time, was stepping *through* the portal like it was nothing more than a hologram and going nowhere at all.

Back in undergrad, it had taken three tries before Ellie had been able to accompany Liam to one of her own memories for the first time. For their adviser, it had taken seven. Over the years they'd worked out something of a system, and determined there were a few things that made it easier to get through the first time. One was mental preparation for what to expect during the jump process. Another was at least some prior acquaintance with Liam.

And so the week before the jump found Ellie once again on the interminable train up to Blossom Heights, this time with her research partner settled in the seat beside her.

"Stella's going to be so excited," she remarked. "You're the one she wanted to meet from the beginning."

Liam shifted, brows pulling together in the slight discomfort he always seemed to have with getting the quasi-celebrity treatment. "She's met me already now, at both the jumps. I'm sure the shine has worn off."

"She got to shake your hand, sure, but she didn't really get to *talk* to you. That seemed to be what she was most interested in, last time I was here." Ellie turned to face him more directly. "If it helps, I don't think she's really interested in *you* exactly, I think it's more what you can do for her. And oh," she added, "heads up, she *is* going to call you a chronomancer. Be nice about it."

He groaned and leaned his head back against the seat. "Better and better. I may have to become terribly ill on this train ride."

"I think Renton would insist on propping you up and dragging you in to see Stella anyway. The jump is next week, you're not getting out of this meeting *that* easily. Just sit back and think about getting cited in Plenisari research papers."

He gave her one of those grins that always made her feel like the suns were coming out from the clouds. "The sacrifices I make to move our field forward."

Nearly an hour later, they were face to face once again with Stella herself. The memorist had lost none of her sharpness in the weeks since Ellie's previous visit, but at least Ellie wasn't the focus of it this time. Stella barely acknowledged her as they settled into the same seats in her suite's cheery living room, instead barraging Liam with questions on what the jump would be like and what they would be able to do once they were in the past. They were all reasonable questions, that anyone might have about going back in time, but Stella focused on Liam's answers with an intensity that reminded Ellie of a bird of prey.

She decided not to share that thought with him later.

"We *will* see Maria, yes? Not just from across the room, but close enough to *actually* see her? Talk with her?"

Liam's brow creased. "Well…we probably will be able to get that close, yes, particularly if we use a memory where you were talking to Maria to anchor the jump. The portal will open in the memory's location, when you and she will still be there. But you have to understand," he added quickly, "*we* won't be able to interact with her. When we travel back in the time stream, we're not a part of it. It's like…" he gestured as if trying to pluck the right words out of the air.

"It's like being a ghost," he said finally. "Or watching an immersive film. You can observe the world around you, but you can't interact with it at all. I'm sorry if that's disappointing."

"It's fine." Stella's expression remained unreadable as always. "As long as we'll see her up close."

Liam glanced over at Ellie, his eyes lingering a half-second on hers. One of the advantages of working closely with your best friend for years was being able to read each other fairly well. And right now, she could read that Liam was picking up on some of the same oddness from Stella that Ellie had on the first visit.

She tilted her head slightly to say *give it your best shot, Tsanara. Maybe she'll talk to* you.

He scooted forward a bit in his seat, leaning in towards Stella. Ellie imagined she could hear the whir of his emergency-defense-charm powering up. "Ms. Hartford, it's wonderful that you're so interested in the mechanics of the jump - *I* certainly think it's a very interesting subject." He gave her one of those sun-behind-the-clouds smiles, as if to cement the idea that they were connected. Stella's face didn't change.

"Tell me, was there something you were hoping to see or do during the jump? As you know this project is very important to the University, and of course we'll be happy to help you any way that we can."

"No grand reasons to concern yourself." Her tone was detached, bordering on dismissive. "I'm ninety-two, I'm at the end of my life, I'd like to see my sister again before my time's up. Even if *seeing* is all I can do."

"Well, we'll certainly be able to provide that opportunity." He leaned back in silent retreat. Stella, it seemed, was impervious to the weaponized puppy eyes. "Since you'll be traveling through the portal with us, the preparations will be slightly different this time…"

For the next hour, Liam walked through what Stella could expect from the jump, the last steps their team was undertaking, and the plan for observing the Address once they arrived. Stella listened politely throughout, occasionally asking questions, and at the end of the meeting bid them a cordial goodbye. They walked back to the train station in silence.

"So it's not just me," Ellie said finally, when they were ensconced on the empty train back towards the city center. "There's something weird here."

"I think so too," Liam agreed heavily. "I didn't get what you meant before, but you're right. All her answers are the *right* answers, it *shouldn't* be weird, but it just feels like something is… off."

He shifted in his seat to face her, dark eyes serious. "But…so far she's given us everything we need from her, that we wouldn't be able to get otherwise. The University's interest in this is getting to Plenisar. So long as Stella can deliver us a memory that gets us back to the Planetary Address, I'm not sure anything else matters here."

"Fair enough," she conceded. "And the last thing we want is to give her any reason to reconsider."

"Exactly. Stella could still pull the plug on this between now and next week, if we upset her." Liam shrugged. "We did our disclosure - if she was hoping to interact with Maria in the past, we told her we can't deliver. If she just wants to see her sister's memory, well, that's the plan anyway. I hope it's enough for whatever she's looking for."

9

The Plenisar jump had occupied nearly all of Ellie's waking thoughts for weeks. Now that it was finally here, she wasn't sure if she wanted to leap with excitement or throw up her breakfast all over the carpet. As the final preparations whirled around her, maybe a bit of both.

They were once again staging from the university, which had at least made setup straightforward. Since there was no physical anchor here anyway, Dahlia had noted, they might as well work from somewhere they didn't have to pay for.

Ellie had to hand it to her - the party plan had come together. Even with all the hours they'd spent in the Archives, uncovering bits and pieces of everyday Plenisar, it had been hard to imagine it all coming to life. But now that she stood in the midst of it, Ellie hardly recognized the space. The formerly anodyne faculty meeting room was transformed into an evocation of the world Stella had left behind.

Hopefully, anyway. The best judge would be Stella herself.

Still, Dahlia had spared no effort. There were vintage advertisements lining the walls, images of long-past products and performances carefully sourced from the Archives. On Plenisar they would have been electronic, of course, not simply printed paper, but hopefully the content itself would at least help. The foods they'd identified were laid out in colorful trays on long tables, and numerous people were standing around with plates as if it really were a party. The top-100 pop playlist provided a peppy soundtrack, piping from their borrowed electronic speaker with a slightly tinny quality.

Such a valuable antique was only allowed outside under the close supervision of an on-site Archivist; Ellie wasn't surprised at all that Mat had finagled his way into the assignment. He waved her over with a broad grin.

"It's actually here. Are you ready?"

"As I'll ever be. Thanks for your help with the music, by the way." She gestured at the little speaker, placed carefully in the center of its small table, away from stray elbows. "Hopefully there haven't been any issues?"

"None at all, my only job here is to make sure nobody spills punch on an irreplaceable Plenisari relic, and all your crew has been giving it wide berth." His lips quirked. "We'll see how I feel after the playlist loops for the third time. 3999's Top 100 Hits all kind of sound the same."

As if to prove his point, the song ended and another began, with a nearly identical beat.

"I'm excited to actually watch you work, though," he commented. "It's kind of amazing just to see what you did with all the records we unearthed."

"This was all Dahlia. I'm always impressed by what she can pull off, usually without a lot of time. Even the costumes." She swished her light-but-voluminous skirt, an almost perfect replica of the image they'd used from the Archives. "Everything fit the first time, and we all look perfect. I wouldn't mind walking down the street in this."

Dahlia herself bustled up to join them then, a plate of cake in one hand.

"This is really good, you two," she announced. "You nailed it on the flour substitution. Whether or not it tastes authentic, I'm calling it a win."

"Speaking of wins, Dahlia, we were just talking about how incredible this set is, you've done amazingly at bringing the whole thing to life."

Dahlia's cheeks pinked, though she couldn't quite hide her grin. "It really came together, didn't it? You know, this job really is like the theatre. We're trying to evoke a feeling in the viewer, get them primed for the performance. The only difference is instead of a play, the performance is ripping a hole in space and time."

Something in her tone made Ellie glance sideways. "Any chance you'd ever want to come with us on a jump?"

Dahlia chortled. "Absolutely not. I'm quite happy staying put in my own spot in the time stream, thanks."

She glanced over at Mat, who gave her an amused shrug. "Maybe someday, but for now I'm with Dahlia on the whole 'leaping through mysterious time portals' thing. You and Liam can be the brave ones, we'll cheer you on from the present day."

"Speaking of," Dahlia cut in, "Ellie, do you mind doing a final check-in with Stella? It's her last chance to change her mind before *she* traverses the mysterious hole in time and space. I know going with you was her big requirement, but she can still back out if it doesn't look quite as fun now that we're actually here."

She glanced pointedly at the mass of wires and devices, centering on the large machine that would send them back to Plenisar. Ellie had done this enough times that the equipment involved barely registered any more in her sight, but now that Dahlia brought it up she could see how the setup could be intimidating.

"I'll go talk to her." Given their previous interviews with Stella, Ellie would be surprised if anything short of a planetary meltdown would stop her from trying to make the jump, but it didn't hurt to check in. "I'll catch up with you both afterward."

After I get back from Plenisar still sounded a bit too impossible to say.

As she turned to go, Mat leaned close to murmur in her ear. "Win one for the Ags, Ellie."

She gave him a nod that felt very much like a salute, and headed over to find Stella.

Unlike the previous jumps, when she had been seated a ways back from the devices, Stella today was situated near the inner ring, her walker at the ready. In the sea of replica costumes, she was wearing the one true vintage piece: a secondary school track team jacket that she had apparently brought over from Plenisar and held on to in the decades since. She watched the preparations with her usual equanimity, no hint of any second thoughts on her face.

"I remember when this song came out when I was in secondary school," she said as Ellie approached. Ellie nearly jumped in surprise at being addressed, but managed to keep her equilibrium as Stella glanced over at her. Compounding her shock, there was a wry humor in Stella's expression. "I thought it was annoying then, and it hasn't gotten any less annoying over a century and a half. Number one on the global charts for three whole weeks, I couldn't get away from it. Still can't, can I?"

"I can ask Matheus to change it-"

"Oh, no need. If I survived it a hundred-odd years ago I'll survive it now. This is a very cute little soiree you all put together." Stella lifted her plate. "You even tried to make me Autumn Cake. That was very sweet of you."

"We found the recipe in the Archives, and tried to recreate it with Altren ingredients. Did we do a good job?"

Stella chuckled. "No. But I could tell that it was *supposed* to be Autumn Cake."

She returned her gaze to Liam, deep in concentration as he adjusted one of the time machine's dials. Like Ellie, his costume had come from the film star photos in the Archives, and Ellie would never admit aloud that he wore those slim-fitting pants and light tailored jacket better than the long-ago Jasen Arcstone ever did.

She gave herself a mental shake. Stella was almost certainly not considering Liam's jacket.

"Are you here to ask if I'm really sure I want to do this? Last chance to change my mind and all that? Would be more convenient for you two, I suppose, not to have me tagging along."

Ellie chose to ignore that last part. "I'm required to ask. But," she added truthfully, "I expected you wouldn't miss it for anything."

"Good girl. Now let's see if your chronomancer is almost ready. These bones will get stiff if I have to sit here too long."

He *was* almost ready, though a tension in his posture belied his outward confidence.

"Everything good?" she asked softly.

"Yes. As good as it's going to be." Liam frowned at the numbers again. Ellie waited. Finally, he glanced back up with a tiny huff of frustration. "It's fine. It's within expected parameters. I'm just not used to having this little visibility into a jump. Usually I can tell you precisely where we're going to come out, but since none of us know anything about where we're going..."

"We'll find out when we get there?" she finished for him.

"Exactly. Per Stella's memory we *should* come out near the Institute for Global Environmental Research in the city of Tancerra, where Maria gave the Address." Liam's sigh sounded resigned. "But since 'Tancerra' is just a name on a map to everyone but Stella, we will indeed find out when we get there."

Another sigh, and he summoned up a smile for her.

"It's good, El. Really. You can tell Stella it's time to start getting ready to go."

A scant fifteen minutes later they were gathered for the jump. Ellie and Stella were positioned on either side of Liam, who held the console at the ready.

"Just like before," he reminded Stella. He was all confidence now, his earlier misgivings buried beneath professional poise. If their memorist was nervous at all, a slight tightness on her knuckles as she gripped her walker was the only sign. "Focus on the most intense memory surrounding the Address, and I'll do the rest."

Stella gave him a tight nod and closed her eyes. Ellie could feel the entire room around them holding their breath as Liam keyed in the sequence, only to erupt in the low buzz of barely-contained excitement as the portal leapt to life. On the other side was the city of Tancerra on Plenisar, 153 years in the past.

Liam caught Ellie's eyes and gave her a nod, then looped the arm that held the console around hers and slipped his free hand through Stella's. They stepped through to an entirely different world.

10

The entirely different world looked remarkably like someone's living room. Ellie blinked, trying to reconcile what she was seeing with what she expected. They were supposed to come out near the Institute where Maria Hartford would shortly begin her now-famous Address.

Unless the Institute was housed in an apartment building, they were in the wrong place.

Liam's eyes darted around them in confusion and some alarm.

"This isn't where we were supposed to come out. The landing site was imprecise, but all my calculations were still that —"

"There's nothing wrong with your calculations." Stella's voice was calm. "We were always going to come out here."

Before they could answer the synchronization completed, and sudden raised voices shattered the pre-sync silence.

"No you aren't, you're *abandoning* us! You don't even care about our family at all!" Teenage Stella abruptly stormed into view from an adjacent hallway. She was crying.

"Stella, you know that's not true." Ellie's breath hitched. It was Maria Hartford *herself* who followed Stella out of the hall.

The Savior of Plenisar was outwardly calm, with only small lines of tension around her eyes betraying any internal struggle as she appealed to her sister. "This is really, really hard, Stella. I wish there was another way. But I can't go with you."

At Stella's stony silence, she continued. "This terraforming project is humanity's best hope for survival, and they want me to lead it. I can't say no, not with so much at stake. Not even if it means giving up going with you. I can't."

"Yes, you can. It's very easy. You just say 'no,' and then you get on the ship to Altren with me and Mom and Dad. Humanity already *has* hope, they have Altren, and we have a chance to go there. And you're ruining *everything* by staying behind."

"Because most people don't have a choice except to stay. Even with all the ships, Altren won't be able to save more than a handful of people. If there's any hope to fix this, it's on Plenisar."

Stella's tears intensified into heaving sobs, anger and sadness at war on her face. "But why does it have to be *you*."

"Because it has to be someone, and I'm the best one for the job," Maria answered gently. "I love you, Stella, very very much. But I can't go with you to Altren. Sometimes..." Maria closed her eyes for a moment. "Sometimes, you have to do things that are bigger than yourself."

She reached out a hand, as if to pull her sister in for a hug. But young Stella squirmed out of her grasp with a hiss. Anger, it seemed, had won out over sadness.

"If you *really cared about me* you wouldn't choose everyone else." Her voice rose in pitch, nearly a scream. "Fine. *Go.* Give your stupid speech. I don't want to hear it. If I'm never going to see you again, then just *leave* already."

She pushed past back down the hallway, slamming a door with enough force to shake the whole apartment. Maria followed and knocked to no response. She tried again, calling quietly through the impassive wood, but there was only silence from the other side.

Ellie had never felt so much like a voyeur in the past as she did then, watching a full range of emotions pass over the Savior of Plenisar's face. Frustration, grief, regret, and finally resignation, as Maria called a quiet goodbye through the doorway and turned away. She collected a bag near the entryway and, with a final look around the apartment that her family would soon vacate, let herself out.

"Quick," their Stella interjected, her tone full of urgency. "We need to follow her."

Liam's face reflected Ellie's own confusion, but Stella was already pushing forward as quickly as she could manage, and they could only follow her down the hallway. But Maria walked at a brisk pace, faster than the current-day Stella could match, and when they finally made it out the building's front doors it was just in time to see her climb into a waiting private car. It was gone before they even reached the curb.

Stella let out a surprisingly colorful string of curses. "We need to find another way to get to the Institute. It's too far to walk."

"Wait, why do we need another way to get there?" Liam was attempting his smooth-professional mode, but a trickle of alarm leaked through. "Can't we just go with your younger self when you go?"

The almost pleading note in his tone matched the churning in Ellie's gut. Something was wrong here, and somehow she knew that whatever Stella said next was going to make it all worse. But it would be really wonderful if, against all odds, Stella had some sort of explanation that meant the mission was going to go to plan after all.

She didn't. "We can't do that," their memorist confirmed. "Because I didn't go."

Liam looked like he'd been struck; Ellie could only assume her expression was much the same.

"I didn't go," Stella repeated. "My parents had already gone ahead. Maria wanted to break the news to me privately, and as you see I refused to go with her. Instead I sat in my bedroom and wallowed in my own hurt and anger, and then in a few hours they came and got me to go into cryosleep. By sundown I was on my way to Altren."

"But…" Ellie hated the plaintive sound in her voice. "But you were so detailed. When we talked about your memory of the Address you could recall *everything*."

Stella made a dismissive motion. "I watched every recording, from every angle, over and over. I remember it better than the people who were *actually* there. But my own living memory ends only in this apartment. I was a stupid kid wrapped up in my own hurt, and it cost me the chance to say goodbye to my sister. The last words I ever said to Maria are the ugly ones you just heard."

She brought a hand down on her walker for emphasis. "Now I'm at the end of my life, and this is the closest I'll ever be able to come to making it right. I might never be able to *actually* tell Maria I'm sorry, but I can say it to her now and hope that maybe wherever she is, she'll know. So we have to follow her."

Liam's brows were drawn tightly together. "This is not what Dr. Nelseren and I agreed to, nor did the University."

Stella looked unimpressed. "You want to witness the Planetary Address? Well, I'm the last one left who can get you anywhere close. You'll never get another chance at this, just like I won't. Work with me, chronomancer, and we can both get what we want."

"Dr. Nelseren and I need to confer on what to do." Liam grabbed Ellie's elbow and started drawing her away, Stella's parting words echoing over his shoulder.

"Decide fast. Or we'll miss the Address just like I did before."

———

"We're so screwed. Everything about this is screwed. This is *so* not the plan we signed on for."

Ellie hadn't seen Liam nervous-babble since they were

preparing for their first thesis defense. She wondered if he realized he'd started to pace.

"What's more, this is *dangerous*." He gestured at the console in his other hand, still serenely displaying their coordinates. "If the Institute is as far away as Stella remembers, then the established safe zone for leaving lived memories isn't nearly big enough to get us from here to there." He met her eyes. "You know what we're *supposed* to do now."

She did. "Per protocol, we're supposed to abort the mission altogether and return home. The mission cannot be completed safely and thus we should return immediately to minimize further risk." They *should*. Certainly. But…

"But Stella's not wrong," she added. "We *won't* get another shot at this. And it's not going to be a good look if we pass it up." Her voice shook a little as the gravity of the situation caught up with her. "For me especially. They're going to ask how this never came out in my interviews with Stella."

"It's not your fault Stella is an amazing liar, El. You didn't cause this. But…yeah." He blew out a frustrated sigh. "It's not going to be good for *either* of our careers. Actually let's be real, if we cancel the mission now we're not going to *have* careers. With what the whole project cost the university, even *Dahlia* will be lucky to get out of this with a job if we call things off now."

Her stomach sank even further. He was right, of course. The university wouldn't fire them for following safety protocol; even Felden likely couldn't manage that with a straight face. But there would be a great deal of questions asked about how things got to this point. Ultimately the grounds for firing them would be for fumbling the advance work, and also quite probably ensuring Stella would never work with the department again.

In short, it would be an unmitigated disaster, someone would need to be blamed for it, and that someone would 100% be Ellie and Liam. Which had consequences beyond themselves.

"It won't just be Dahlia," she said softly. "They'll probably shut down AUTDRI altogether. Felden already thinks it's a waste of time. And without you, they've got nothing to do."

He didn't disagree. "We worked so hard for this. We spent the last *four years* working for this. And now it's all going off the rails."

As she watched Liam pace, the knot in her stomach grew. She knew this work was hugely important to him, knew that he would be devastated to lose AUTDRI and the chance to pursue the field. But she also knew he'd land on his feet. He'd be miserable. His parents would probably be awful about it. But as humiliating as failure here would be, the Tsanara family's business interests left him plenty to fall back on.

She had nothing to fall back on. She was qualified for a teaching role, but if AUTDRI was shut down because of her and Liam, she was likely to be blacklisted from University jobs altogether. Shana *might* be able to help her get an interview at the secondary school, but even then, such a spectacular disaster in such a high-profile field was likely to follow her anywhere in Altren City that she tried to go. And she hardly had the funds to try to wait out the scandal.

No, if they failed here, she was likely to end up right back where she started in the Agsteads. *Win one for the Ags*, Mat had whispered, but she was going to do the opposite. She was going to lose so badly, it would be *harder* for the ones that came after her. She was going to make things worse for every Agstead kid that dreamed of more in the city.

That snapped her out of the spiral. Ellie was not going to surrender the life she'd built for herself, the dreams she'd worked for, the difference she'd hoped to make, because Stella Hartford had lied about her past. If it was all going to end badly, she was at least going to go down fighting.

"Okay." She drew in a breath. "Panicking is not helping us. We need to look at our options."

It came out harsher than she intended, but Liam stopped pacing and turned to face her. She plowed ahead.

"Option 1, we follow protocol, we abort the mission and go back empty-handed. Maybe we do some observation around this area and everyday life on Plenisar so we can bring *something* back to the University, but it wouldn't be what we came for and it wouldn't be why they funded this mission in the first place. Most likely, we get fired and AUTDRI gets shut down." *And I spend the rest of my life planting potatoes in disgrace*, but she kept that part to herself. He wouldn't understand, and they didn't have time to argue about it.

Liam shook his head. "Not the option we want to go with, if we have any kind of choice."

"Agreed. Option 2, we go after the mission anyway." She looked over at him. "You know better than I do what that means."

Liam's brows drew together. "Sort of. The truth is that nobody *really* knows. The safety zone is a one-and-a-half kilometer radius from the portal because that's the furthest anyone has gone, and we *know* you can go that far without a problem. We don't know how much further past that you can go before there *is* a problem. It could be quite a ways." His eyes turned thoughtful. "Nobody knows because nobody wants to find out the hard way."

"High risk, high reward, then. Option 3..." she paused, wracking her brain. "I don't think there is an Option 3, actually. It's go big or go home." She drew a deep breath. "I vote go big."

Silence for a moment, then he lifted his eyes to hers.

"I do too. There's risk. We could end up trapped here, or worse. No one actually knows what happens if the portal destabilizes while we're on the other side. But we also don't know if the portal will even be affected at all. It could be totally fine." He sounded like he was trying to convince himself as much as her. "We'd be essentially leaving the established boundary and seeing what happens. If we pull it off, we'd be breaking new ground on the safety zone."

"So to summarize, either we return in triumph with even

more data than we promised, or it's a complete disaster and we find out what happens when a time portal breaks with us inside it." A smile tugged at her lips in spite of herself. "Sounds like either way, we're going to get cited in a lot of papers."

Liam's lips curved in a hint of his usual grin. "When you put it like that, it's win-win, right?" More seriously, he added. "And I really want to see this through. I know you do too."

She did. Even beyond what it meant for her career and her future. Ellie came here to see the Planetary Address, and she wanted to *actually* see it. More than that, this was the only chance she'd ever get to see Plenisar. Humanity's birthplace, a whole different planet, available up close for this last narrow window and then never again.

That was worth taking some risks.

"Then let's go tell Stella the good news," she answered, more confidently than she felt. "We've still got a speech to catch."

11

Even with everything going sideways, stepping out into the streets of Tancerra still took her breath away. The Hartford family's apartment had just looked like, well, an apartment. It wouldn't have been out of place in a building on Altren. Out on the streets, however, they were truly in another world.

The sky was a different color, a deep almost-violet rather than Altren's pale blue. There was also only a single sun, looking somewhat lonely hanging in the sky. Then there was the air.

Once in her childhood in West Ag 3, lightning had struck a nearby forest, and set off a raging inferno that belched thick, choking smoke into the sky. The acrid stench was seared in her memory, along with the way the smoky air had burned in her lungs. The air around them now had that same burn, but here there was nothing on fire.

She'd read about the polluted air of Plenisar, of course, and how it contributed to shortened lifespans among the Plenisari of the late 4th millennia. Intellectually she understood, should have expected it. But actually experiencing it herself was still unnerving. At least they wouldn't be here long enough for any lasting effects.

Hopefully. And if the portal collapsed, well, long-term air pollution exposure would probably be the least of their worries.

In any case, there was no time for sightseeing. They needed to figure out how to get to the Institute in time to see Maria give the Address, or all of this would be for nothing no matter *what* they did.

"So Stella," she started, "Where are we, and do you know how far it is to where we're going?"

"Too far to walk, even if I were a spry young thing like you two. It must be…oh, at least eight or nine kilometers, if I'm remembering right. Even if you were to leave me behind and walk for hours to get there," she looked at them sternly over her glasses, as if daring them to say they'd considered it, "the speech would be over by the time you did. We need to find a ride."

She took in the space around them, muttering to herself. "Now where *was* that bus stop…"

Ellie exchanged glances with Liam again. "Stella remembers how to find a bus stop from 80 years ago on another planet" was not a dependency they'd considered.

Their memorist was still talking, though Ellie got the impression it was half to them and half to herself. "I didn't take the bus often, back in the day. Usually I had private transport to school and back, and too much walking around outside wasn't good for anyone's health. Wasn't like on Altren, where everything's clean.

"And towards the end," she acknowledged with a dark glance down the street, "the city wasn't all that safe. Turns out when the world is ending, the social contract starts breaking down too. Still, in this part of town the things were usually OK. Sometimes I'd go out with friends when a ride wasn't available, and we'd take the bus, and to get down there I would go…" she narrowed her eyes and pointed down a street. "I'd go this way, past the grocery and the park. It was a nexus stop, most of the city lines stop there. We'll be able to find something to get us near the Institute. Let's go, children. Time's wasting." She set off down the street without waiting.

Stella's mobility set a slow pace, but that meant they had plenty of time to look around. Not *everything* on Plenisar was unfamiliar. The architecture around them reminded Ellie of home, at least in the broad strokes. The shape of the structures, the placement of the windows, the elements of their facades - if one of the nearby buildings were suddenly teleported to Altren City, the only thing noticeably out of place would be how dirty it was.

It was mildly disappointing, in that they'd come all the way through time and space just to see the same things they had at home, but it made sense. Much of Altren City had been remotely constructed by robotics during this same period, while the ships carrying its future residents made the long journey through space. It still felt weird to see the same buildings here, so like home yet not.

The sight was stirring up memories for Stella, however. As they slowly made their way towards the bus stop, she pointed out various spots and told stories about how they'd figured into her childhood. It was more forthcoming about her private life than she'd ever been in their prep sessions. Part of Ellie wanted to believe they'd crossed some sort of relationship barrier with Stella, that she felt comfortable now opening up; the rest of her suspected Stella just wanted to talk through this, and they were the only ones available.

It was fascinating regardless. After the first few minutes, she quietly got out her notebook and started scribbling. Ellie had never been more grateful to herself for putting in the effort to learn how to walk and write simultaneously.

The bus stop wasn't far, by objective standards, but with Stella's limited mobility it still took them much longer to get there than Liam and Ellie could have managed alone. Still, they had time: according to Liam's console, there was more than an hour left before Maria was scheduled to begin the Address. It wasn't a *huge* margin, and she would have been more comfortable with another hour just in case. But they were close to the station now, and a competent bus system should still get them to the Institute with time to spare.

It was distance readings that Liam was more focused on.

"How are we doing?" Ellie asked quietly.

"Still in the safety zone. We've only gone about half a kilometer from the portal. Once we get on the bus, though…" He forced a smile at her, though worry tinged his expression. For all his earlier determination, Liam had clearly spent the walk thus far thinking about everything that might go wrong. "Well, we'll find out real quick if we're going to be heroes or a cautionary tale."

She gave him a smile back that she hoped was encouraging. "Advancing science either way, right?"

"Yeah." He gave a shaky laugh. "The worst part if this goes wrong is going to be how insufferable my parents would be. They'd probably bring up at the funeral how they always told me to go into Material Science instead anyway."

Ellie's throat grew tight. She didn't want to think about her parents at her funeral. They'd always been so *proud* of her, for everything she'd been able to do beyond the Agsteads. The thought of how devastated they'd be, if those same achievements led to her death, was almost more distressing than the thought of actually dying.

Although she'd like to avoid that too.

Fortunately, she was rescued from having to formulate a response by their arrival at the bus station. She shoved the dark thoughts away - either it would happen or it wouldn't - and resolutely shifted focus to the here and now.

In what Ellie was beginning to think of as Plenisar's signature character, the bus station was dirty and a bit run down, but had clearly been nice at one time. The large plastic canopy shading its rows of seats was artfully molded with a graceful pattern of waves that Ellie might have described as 'whimsical,' but years or decades under the sun had turned it brittle and cracked. There were still a few seats with padding, but most were heavily damaged by some combination of wear or vandalism. Naturally, everything was coated in a thin layer of grime.

Some of her thoughts must have shown on her expression.

"There wasn't much money for investment in Plenisar at this point," Stella noted. "Everything was either going towards Altren or the terraforming project. This was actually one of the better neighborhoods, you know. If you go to some of the poorer parts of the city, things get very bad very quickly. But you'll have to take my word for it," she added, scanning the station. "We have places to go and people to see."

The station's route map was semi-obscured behind a weathered, heavily scratched pane of clear plastic that had probably been intended to protect it from the elements, and even the parts that Ellie *could* make out seemed borderline incomprehensible. Stella leaned in to study it more intently.

"Forgot how complicated the Tancerra Municipal lines could get," she muttered. "And it's been a very long time since I was here and riding the bus. But as I recall, the Institute should be over…." Her finger hovered in a line over the dirty plastic before stabbing triumphantly towards a cluster of symbols. "There. The Red Line will take us within a block of where we need to go. And it should be here…soon." Stella lips curved in a satisfied smile; Ellie abruptly realized she'd never seen Stella smile before this. "Ten minutes. We should make it in plenty of time."

It was a long ten minutes. Ellie tried to take advantage by sketching the bus station and its environment; she even tried to get down a copy of the bus route map, though her rendition ended up even more of a chaotic mess than the original. Liam paced and kept glancing at his console. Stella settled down on one of the few intact seats and seemed content to just sit and wait, until she spoke again into the silence.

"I wonder if any of this is still here." She looked around again, though her gaze seemed far away. "Over one hundred and fifty years, since I last stood here. If I saw Tancerra again, the *now* Tancerra, would I recognize it?"

She didn't seem to expect a response; in fact, Ellie wasn't sure she was talking to them at all. For a moment Stella *looked* old, as if some of the vitality that Ellie associated with her had dimmed. For a moment, too, her expression changed to something more pensive, and Ellie wondered if she was starting to have second thoughts about her plan to try and get closure for what had happened with Maria. But then the Red Line 518 pulled up to the curb, and there was no time for any of them to reconsider.

———

The bus ride was surreal. It wasn't crowded, so they had no trouble finding seats, but the few other people on the bus couldn't see them anyway. It really was like being a ghost.

Ellie would have said she was used to it by now, with how many time jumps she and Liam had made together, but the bus reminded her of their earliest trips and the discomfiting feeling of being invisible. This was the longest and most involved trip either of them had ever made, and there was still the looming possibility of falling off the figurative map. She supposed it made sense to be a bit nonplussed.

Once again, she tried to distract herself by sketching the interior of the bus, and the ordinary Plenisari people sitting further down. Every one of those people, she realized uncomfortably, were dead in her own time.

Liam sat beside her, eyes glued to the console. Ellie was not a temporal physicist, obviously, but to her inexpert eyes it looked the same as it always did.

"What are you watching for?" she asked softly. There was no need to actually whisper, no one but Stella could hear them anyway, but the force of habit was strong.

"Anything to change," he answered, his voice quiet as well. "So far so good, the parameters aren't showing any anomalies. But I don't know if there would be. That's the whole thing here, right? Nobody does. But we're going to find out soon."

He gestured towards one of the indicators, a number that was continuously ticking up. "There's our distance from the portal. When it hits 1.5 km, we're breaking new ground. One way or another."

It was at 1 km. Then 1.2. They both watched it tensely as it reached 1.4, then 1.5, then 1.6. 1.7.

The portal's stability readings were unchanged.

They both exploded in almost giddy sighs of relief.

Ellie leaned over to murmur in his ear. "Look at us, only three months on the job and we're already breaking new ground for science."

Liam grinned back at her. "And maybe even making it back to tell the tale." He glanced back quickly at the console, as if to reassure himself the readings were still steady. "There's still a chance every step could be too far, but it didn't immediately collapse, which gives me hope that it won't collapse at all. The readings are all still good. And this is going to make for an incredible paper when we get back."

"How about *Breaking All The Rules: An Exploration of Increased Portal Stability Awareness Through Reckless Disregard for Personal Safety*?" she suggested. Liam pretended to think.

"I don't know, I like *Tragedy to Triumph: How Not Knowing When to Quit Turned a Fiasco into a Success*, but we can consider your idea too."

Before she could respond, the bus lurched to a creaking halt, a barely-discernible muttering over the intercom announcing their stop.

"This is it," Stella announced, getting carefully to her feet. Ellie and Liam followed, and they disembarked a short ways away from a large, crowded building. The bus pulled away with a groan, and there was nowhere to go but forward to what they'd come here to do.

12

The Institute for Global Environmental Research rose majestically from further down the street. Like everything they'd seen on Plenisar it was a bit worn, but it managed to look dignified instead of rundown.

It was also a hive of activity as a crowd of people swarmed around the gates set up outside the entrance, waiting to be admitted to the auditorium. It seemed like every media outlet on the continent had arrived to hear what the new head of the Institute's moonshot terraforming project had to say.

Security was tight as well. Ellie wished they had time for a sketch or two, but had to content herself with frantic scribbled descriptions as they drew up to the front of the long line and reached the multiple layers of metal detectors and explosive-sniffing dogs. *That* part had never made it into any of their learning materials about the Planetary Address. She was suddenly reminded of Stella's words about the social contract breaking down.

Naturally, they bypassed the security stations and simply walked in. Being a ghost had its advantages.

Maria's office was listed on the directory, just down the hall. The door was ajar when they got there, and Ellie's breath caught as they slipped inside. Standing by the window, with her back to them, was Maria.

The Savior of Plenisar stared out the window with an impassive expression that reminded Ellie of Stella. She seemed lost in thought as she gazed through the thick-paned glass, as if watching something they couldn't see.

Stella shuffled forward and began to speak.

"Maria, I'm so sorry. I said all that today because I was hurt and silly, and I didn't mean any of it, but by the time I got my head on straight to apologize it was too late and you were gone. I've carried that regret with me for the last eighty years of my life. Well, I guess it would be a hundred and fifty years for you, wouldn't it?"

Maria didn't react, of course, because she couldn't hear her. Just as they'd told Stella at the start of all this. But this was something Stella needed to do for herself, wasn't it?

"Here's what I should have said instead," Stella continued. "Maria, I'm so proud of you. I know now how hard you fought to get here, how much drive it took to be the one entrusted with saving humanity. I understand now that the choice to stay was probably the hardest thing in your life, and," her voice grew thick "you made the *right* choice."

Stella moved closer to stand beside her, staring out the same glass. "When that ship finally landed on Altren, the universe I woke up to was so much better than the one I had left. All the scarcity and disaster we grew up with was just old stories to people, because you had the courage to stay. These kids with me don't have to live with the burden of being the last, because you had the courage to stay. There are *billions of people* alive and thriving here on Plenisar, because you had the courage to stay."

She took a few more steps forward then, so that she was nearly between Maria and the window. "I hope you knew, despite how we parted, that I loved you very much. You'll always be my sister. And I'm so proud that it was *your* hands that guided us to a better future."

Maria blinked and looked up suddenly, as if she'd heard an unexpected sound. The air *whooshed* out of Ellie's lungs. She met Liam's eyes quickly and saw her own shock reflected there. Had they just seen what they thought they saw? It couldn't be, it shouldn't be *possible*.

It was gone in a flash, a fraction of a second, then Maria returned her gaze to the window. The whole moment was over so quickly, Ellie wasn't sure if she'd even really seen anything at all.

A knock at the door interrupted any further questions. A voice called softly that it was almost time, Maria was needed backstage. Maria gave a final nod through the window to the sky her family would soon disappear into, and turned and strode out the door without looking back.

Stella watched her go. Her eyes were bright with unshed tears, but the gloom that had been gathering since the bus station was gone. She turned to them with a nod of her own.

"All right. Thank you. Let's go watch your speech."

———

The auditorium was packed with standing room only. The back of the hall was a forest of large cameras and recording equipment, emblazoned with over a dozen different logos. Further up was a sea of suits and notebooks, all standing ready for Maria to take the stage.

Stella shuffled back towards the recording crew, easing herself down to a seat on top of a crate of sound equipment. She waved them forward. "I don't need the best seat in the house, I've watched this enough times *I* could give the speech. Go get what you came for, I'll be here afterward."

Ellie didn't need to be told twice. She slipped into the crowd between two waiting journalists and started dodging her way towards the front, trusting Liam to follow her. If they were truly a part of the crowd, this would have been impossible - or at least, would have garnered a great deal of dirty looks. But once again, being a ghost had its advantages. The assembled people remained completely unaware as Ellie squeezed into a space near the front, Liam a half-second behind her.

"We did it," he murmured in her ear, voice low though there was no one to hear them. "We're actually here. Did you think we'd make it?"

She was about to respond that of course she did, which was only partially a lie, when the doors on the stage opened and Maria Hartford took the podium. A burst of excited chatter from the crowd around them faded to anticipatory quiet, and with a grave nod of acknowledgement Maria began her Address.

They'd already seen it, of course. The recordings were carefully preserved in the national archives of Plenisar and Altren both, and studying the Address was a regular part of secondary school education. Ellie had seen it recently even, had watched the recordings several times in the preceding weeks as part of her preparation for the project. At this point, the words and even Maria's delivery were utterly familiar.

It was still electrifying to watch live. There was a certain distance in the recordings. It was a distance of both time and space, with a camera lens and fifteen decades and a steady buildup of legend separating them from Maria. Here, it was just her, full of hope and determination and charisma.

And uncertainty, though none showed in her demeanor. She was speaking now at the beginning of the terraforming project, with no way to know that it would actually work. No one in this room could know that it would succeed - in fact, Ellie knew from the writings they produced that most of the people assembled in this room assumed it wouldn't. Here and now, Maria Hartford was not a legend in the flesh. She was just a woman who'd had humanity's future thrust on her shoulders, and was going to do her very damn best.

Even knowing that Maria would succeed, that Plenisar and all its multitudes would be saved, tears welled against her lashes as she listened. From his expression, Liam was just as affected. When his hand found hers, she squeezed it back, and knew there was no one she'd rather be experiencing this alongside.

The speech ended, and thunderous applause filled the auditorium. Cameras flashed and questions from the crowd started up almost immediately, but Maria only gave an apologetic wave as she headed off the stage.

"I'm afraid I have to get back to the lab. There's much to do, and not a moment to waste."

She waved again and disappeared out the door at the rear of the stage, and into history.

The buzz of conversation rose up from the crowd around them, but they'd gotten what they came for. They found Stella still seated by the cameras, gaze distant as she watched the empty stage.

"Well," she said finally. "That's that."

13

The portal was where they'd left it in the Hartford apartment. Former apartment, rather - Stella and her family were gone, already preparing for the frozen deep sleep that would take them to Altren.

Maybe it was just in Ellie's head, but the space already felt abandoned, for all that it had been only hours since the family's departure. The shadows seemed heavier now, and not just because the sun had dropped below the adjacent building's roofline. It felt as though they had overstayed their welcome somehow, like the space had played its part and was eager for them to be gone.

That was silly, of course - it was only an empty apartment. Still, Ellie wondered how long they could actually stay, and what might happen if they did. Would they just sit here like ghosts, and watch whoever moved into the apartment next? Would the portal collapse at some point, or simply endure unchanging until someone closed it?

Perhaps someday another field team would answer that question. She was happy it wouldn't be them.

Stella had been quiet on the journey back to the portal, only directing them to the right bus line before retreating into her own thoughts. It was a different quiet than the way in, however. Where before her quiet had held a weary tension, now she sat back with an almost relaxed air. Whatever inner struggle had pushed her to seek out this pseudo-reunion with Maria, it seemed she had conquered it at the Institute. Cliche as it might be to call her "at peace," Ellie thought the description fit.

In contrast to Stella's calm equilibrium, Liam had been almost giddy with relief when they passed through the door to find the portal unchanged. The handheld console had continuously asserted that all was well with the portal, but apparently there was no substitute for seeing it with his own eyes. He started scribbling down readings that were gibberish to Ellie's eyes, but doubtlessly important. One series of arcane symbols was underlined several times.

Finally he snapped his notebook shut and took a deep breath. "I've got everything I need," he announced with a note of finality. His eyes met Ellie's. "Anything left to do before we make the return jump?"

"No," she answered. "I got as much as I could on the way here. I have everything we came for. I feel good about leaving it here." A small pang of regret ran through her at the words, only partially true. There was so much here that she hadn't seen, would never see, and once this door closed it could never open again. But she could stay forever and never see it all. She'd gotten everything they'd needed for the project and then some. It was time to go home.

He turned to Stella. "Anything else before…?"

"No." Her answer was steady. "Thank you for asking. But I left this place behind a very long time ago."

What was there left to say, after that? Liam twined his fingers around Ellie's and offered Stella his arm, and the three of them stepped forward into the portal. The familiar sensation of the crossing washed over her, and Plenisar vanished forever behind them.

———

Altren had scarcely rematerialized around them before they were swarmed by the rest of the team, Dr. Renton at the head of the throng.

"Oh praise the *suns*," she snapped, "You're all in one piece. When the readings showed you leave the safe zone I nearly worried myself to death." Her tone did not sound at all worried, instead sounded absolutely furious, and Ellie realized belatedly that Liam's console had probably triggered all kinds of alarms on this side of the portal. Certainly everyone *else* looked worried.

Oh dear. They hadn't thought that part through. Though given the options they'd had, she wouldn't have done it any differently. Hopefully once Renton saw what they'd come back with, she wouldn't be *too* upset.

Liam was smiling warmly in response, emergency-defense-charm on full overdrive. "I'm sorry we caused you any concern, Director. There was a small hiccup on the ground on Plenisar, but we were able to work around it and fulfill our objectives. And," he added, gesturing at the console in what *almost* felt like a bribe, "I'm pleased to share that we uncovered significant new information about the stability safe zone."

"By running headfirst out of it and seeing what happened." But her grumble had lost its bite, and Ellie didn't miss how her eyes flicked to the console and its promise of groundbreaking new data. She sighed, sounding tired. "But all right. We're all relieved you're back safely. We *will* discuss this later," she held both of their eyes in turn, "but for now let's clean up and go home. It's been a very long day for everyone."

It *had*, and Ellie could feel it waiting to catch up with her the moment they stopped moving. But that moment wasn't quite yet. As the crowd around them started to disperse to various tasks, she released Liam's hand - realized she was still *holding* Liam's hand, and that was certainly not a thought for right now - and went to make herself useful.

She was relieved that cleanup had already started before their return; there wasn't much need to set the stage for a jump that was already underway, and so no need to *really* wait until they'd returned. Privately, she wondered if at least some of the team hadn't been sure they *would* return, once the alarms started up. And if that had been the case, who wanted to hang around and clean up a party after their coworkers had been lost in an unprecedented temporal catastrophe?

She felt a wriggle of guilt then, because judging from the reactions of the rest of their teams - and the hugs she got from Dahlia and Mat, neither of whom were generally the hugging type - everyone *had* been frightened for them. And maybe now that they were back safely, she could admit that it had been just a teensy bit reckless to go ahead.

She still would have made the same decision. Guilt or no, the stakes were too high for anything less. Still, she threw herself into helping with cleanup. It felt like a minor apology.

She was boxing up the last of the advertising posters when one of the research assistants tapped her shoulder. Stella was about to leave, and she wanted to say goodbye to Ellie and Liam before she went.

Ellie found Liam already there, making small talk with Stella as she was helped into a waiting transport. Once she was situated in the seat, she gave them a nod.

"I guess that's everything now, isn't it? Thank you both for your help. I mean it."

Ellie inclined her head, and Liam opened his mouth to respond, probably with some appropriate platitude about how much they'd enjoyed working with her. Stella wasn't finished, however.

"And also?" Her lips quirked as she flicked her eyes between them. "Take it from an old woman, you only get one chance at life and regret is miserable. Whatever reason you think you can't, you'll realize it was silly when you're old and alone and thinking back on your life."

She shut the door without another word, leaving them to stare after the transport as it pulled away.

Liam coughed slightly. "Well that was, ah, cryptic." He couldn't quite meet her eyes. "Maybe we-"

Whatever he was going to say then was lost, as they were interrupted by another assistant urgently requesting Dr. Tsanara's attention. He gave an almost-imperceptible sigh and turned to go, glancing quickly over his shoulder.

"Wait for me? I don't think this will take too long."

It absolutely would take too long, it always did, but she'd wait anyway. Cleanup had wound down and most of the team was leaving, except for the small group conferring with Liam on something technical. Ellie found a seat that wasn't too uncomfortable to work on organizing her notes. She also had messages waiting from her parents and from Kira and Shana both, demanding to know how it had gone, but all she could manage at the moment was a quick note that they'd been successful and a promise to fill them in with all the details tomorrow. When Liam finally emerged nearly a half-hour later, they were the last ones out of the building.

It was late enough that the metro station was empty except for Liam and Ellie, and once the train finally pulled up there were only a handful of other people onboard. Ellie flopped into the closest seat to the door, and Liam collapsed with a groan into the seat beside her.

"That," he asserted vehemently, "was a *day*."

"Agreed." Now that it was all over, the weight of everything that had happened since she woke up that morning seemed to hit her all at once. "I have never been so excited to go home and go to bed. And it's only our third month." She tilted her head back and closed her eyes. "Not sure how we're going to top this for *next* year's performance review."

His laugh was laced with exhaustion, but still warmed her veins. "I'm sure Renton will come up with another impossible task. Maybe we'll pioneer using a robotic memory core to generate a portal, and end up somewhere in the early surveying days."

"At least we'd probably get more than three months to pull something like *that* together."

It was quiet for a moment, both of them lost in their own thoughts. This time, Ellie was the one to speak first.

"When Stella was talking…to Maria…" she paused, unsure of how to say it. It sounded so fantastical to put in words, when everyone *knew* it wasn't possible to affect the past they observed. And yet. "Did you see anything, like…"

"Like Maria reacting in the moment as if she heard her?" He lifted his head and met Ellie's eyes. "Yeah. I did. And if you hadn't seen it too I would think I imagined the whole thing."

"I'm not sure *what* I saw," she admitted. "It *looked* like Maria heard her, or heard *something* at least. We both know it's impossible, but…"

"But we both saw it," Liam finished. "Or we both *thought* we saw it. It was over so quickly I wasn't sure."

"Do you think we should put it in the report?"

His brow furrowed. "If it *did* happen, it's a huge deal. I don't know. It still sounds fake, and neither of us are sure what we saw. Maybe we both just reacted to the suggestion."

"We could add a note, at least," she suggested. "Explain that it's likely a false alarm, but still. It's something future teams could be on the lookout for. "

"Or we could just sound even crazier than the people who rattle on about *chronomancy*. But you're right, it *was* weird and we *did* both notice it. Ugh." He closed his eyes again. "Decide later? After sleep and coffee?"

"*Definitely* after sleep and coffee." The only decision she felt qualified to make right then was whether to bother brushing her teeth before collapsing into bed.

"Speaking of…" Liam pinked slightly, looking uncharacteristically awkward. "I know sleeping in probably sounds amazing right now and I totally get it if you'd rather do that, but…Sunrise

Bread's new seasonal pastries drop tomorrow, and if we get there when they open they'll be fresh out of the oven. Might be fun. To celebrate that we didn't die and everything."

"That does sound fun," she agreed. "And for fresh Sunrise pastries, I think I could manage to set an alarm. To celebrate that we didn't die?"

He shifted. "And…because I see you every day at work, but it feels like we never hang out any more? And I miss you?"

Something clicked in the fog of her mind then, Stella's words and his sudden awkwardness and the sense that there was something else to this.

"Liam…" she started slowly, "are you asking me out?"

His blush intensified. "Do you want me to be? Because if you don't then I'm definitely not doing that."

Laughter bubbled up in her then, only slightly exasperated. "You're impossible, Tsanara."

The question remained though - *did* she want it? There were plenty of reasons to say no, plenty of complications that could arise from a further intertwining of their personal and professional lives. But there was also no denying the lightness in her chest at the question, the way his hand in hers simply felt *right*.

And maybe Stella had a point about only getting one chance to live.

"I don't *not* want it," she answered finally. Emboldened, she slid her fingers through his. "And I think I like the idea, even if it takes some getting used to. Let's just take it a day at a time, eh?" The metro dinged softly, its pleasant synthetic announcer informing them that they were about to arrive at Liam's stop. "See you for pastries tomorrow morning?"

"Outside Sunrise at opening, on the dot." He gave her hand a quick squeeze and hopped off the seat as the train lurched to a full stop, managing to meet her eyes with one of those dazzling smiles. "Looking forward to it, Ellie."

He disappeared off the train, leaving Ellie alone in the car. She settled back to wait through the last few stops. As she gazed out the windows into the evening dark, it finally sunk in that they truly *had done it*. She'd made it to Plenisar and back to tell the tale. They'd broken new ground in understanding the portals, and brought back data that even Plenisar would have to take note of. She'd done something no girl from the Agsteads had ever done before. And…she was seeing Liam for pastries tomorrow, and whatever else came next.

She grinned all the way back to her apartment.

THANK YOU FOR READING!

If you liked this book, please consider leaving a review on Amazon or your favorite review site! Reviews really do make a huge difference in helping indie books find their audience.

To keep up with what's next for Ellie and Liam, you can follow me online, or join my newsletter at lenaalisonknight.com.

ALSO BY LENA ALISON KNIGHT

The Practical Historian's Guide to Time Travel

The Last Window to the Old World

The Gift of the Stars

The Stars Within

The Stars Unbound

The Stars Ablaze

ABOUT THE AUTHOR

Lena Alison Knight grew up reading space opera and high fantasy, and started writing her own as soon as she could hold a crayon steady. She lives with her husband in the San Francisco Bay Area, and when not writing she can be found taking brisk walks, haunting local coffee shops, or sprawled on the couch playing video games.

Lena can be found online at lenaalisonknight.com. Join her newsletter to get a free Gift of the Stars novelette, and keep up with what's coming next.

* 9 7 9 8 9 8 5 4 8 7 2 4 4 *